FIRES IN THE NIGHT

FIRES in the NIGHt

A NOVEL OF LOVE and LEGEND

DAVID MACKEY

PORT HOLE PUBLISHING
Florence, Oregon

ISBN-10: 1-943119-13-9
ISBN-13: 978-1-943119-13-4

Published by:
Port Hole Publishing
179 Laurel St. - Suite D
Florence, Oregon 97439
Ph: 541-999-5725

Dedicated to the late Chad (Leslie) Stitt whose self-loading log truck provided the springboard for this book, and for his hours of teaching me what a gypo logger really does for a living.

CHAPTER 1

Mac was a logger. Every inch a logger. He stood just over six feet six inches tall. As he put it, taller than most but shorter than some. The last time he weighed himself on his doctor's scale he'd picked up at a garage sale for $5, he balanced out at 255 pounds. Not bad for someone with a 45-inch chest and a 38-inch waist. Especially since he was pushing his 35th birthday. He kept his curly red hair short, so short it waved more than curled. He liked jeans, red flannel plaid shirts and red suspenders.

For all his brawn, Mac was a contented, gentle giant. He raised most of his own vegetables and most of his own fruit. He didn't have the patience or time to can it all, so by October one large freezer was full of his own produce. During hunting season, he usually took a deer and an elk and butchered a cow. Those he cut up, wrapped and stuffed in his other not-quite-so-large freezer.

He logged his own place, a little over 350 acres about 15 miles or so up Beaver Creek. This Beaver Creek flows into the Pacific Ocean about 10 miles south of Newport, Oregon. He liked living out there, Douglas fir and hemlock fairly carpeted his hills. He'd spend a week or two in selected areas cruising his timber, selecting his harvest. Then he'd spend a week cutting. When he'd fallen the trees he wanted, he'd take his D-4 Caterpillar tractor up one of the logging roads that laced his property, drag the logs to a landing, load his truck and haul to the mill. His cull logs usually ended up in nearby Toledo to be turned into paper pulp. Saw logs he hauled two hours south to a sawmill at Mapleton. Peelers, high grade logs for making plywood, he hauled two hours north and east to Willamina and the plywood mill there. It made no difference to him, pay was the same and he liked driving his log truck.

Mac's log truck stirred the envy of the local loggers. It wasn't new. In fact, the old, forest-green Kenworth self-loader was probably 15 years old. But it was paid for, clean, comfortable and purred. The only trim on the truck was one line of gold script centered on each door. He'd paid good money for the best sign painter in Newport to embellish his truck with "Mac's Truck." No one teased him about it more than once.

When his roads were too muddy to haul over and the weather too wet and cold to cruise, he tinkered with that truck. He could make it to Willamina and back on less fuel than any other log truck driver on the Oregon coast. He made better time with more logs over the summit on the Van Duzer Corridor section of Highway 18 than anyone else.

Sometimes he tinkered with his friends' log trucks too. But by the end of the next summer, they roared noisily like all the rest. Except Mac's, of course.

He worked by the seasons and flowed with the natural rhythms of the world around him. He'd probably gone on like that until he couldn't lift a chain saw or throw a wrapper, chains that hold down a load of logs, if it hadn't been for a pair of females. He knew one was female as soon as he laid eyes on her. The other one he wasn't sure about until much later.

He caught sight of the first female in church one Sunday. Just about every week he made it into Newport for church. He drove there in his second favorite truck, a 1958 GMC three-quarter-ton pickup with a short, narrow bed. It, too, was paid for, clean, comfortable, purred and was forest green. The gold script in the center of its doors read "Mac's Little Truck."

Anyway, this Sunday in August, he'd put on a short-sleeve white shirt, a clean pair of jeans without patches, white socks that matched his shirt and a pair of brown hush puppies. He'd considered his red velour tie but knew the pastor's wife never approved of it. She'd once said it clashed with his white socks.

Mac sat in one of the back three rows, so he never blocked anyone else's view. This particular morning he was distracted by the back of a lady's head. Not that the back of her head was anything distinctive. But that's probably what caught Mac's attention. When they stood to sing, he looked at the back of her head. With most people, he looked at the top of their heads. She stood beside an older couple who looked a little like her, so, he presumed they were her parents. That didn't make a lot of sense to him either, she looked over 30, but younger than he was.

This lady's face was plain. Her hair was golden, the color of straw that he puts in his barn every fall for bedding for his critters. It fell straight past her shoulders with wisps escaping and floating in the air.

With the end of the service, Mac stayed where he was in the back, watching others greet the trio. The rest of her was pretty plain too, he had to admit. Her shape as viewed from behind didn't hold a whole lot of promise either. Her slender waist curved smaller than her chest or hips but not much. She had a long, narrow face, angular jaw line.

But those eyes. Blue eyes, blue like the ocean on a summer day, when viewed from a cliff high above its surface. Eyes that looked like there was a lot of person behind them. Like the ocean, you could never tell how deep from just the surface. The rest of her? He smiled to himself, only the fastest roads were straight, the best roads always have a few curves. Then those eyes locked onto his. He smiled and so did she.

While quiet and shy are often synonymous to many people, they weren't to Mac. He waited, watching, until the trio was almost beside him, working their way to the exit. His eyes met those blue eyes again and they smiled. Mac motioned for her to step out of the center aisle into the row beside him. She did and he realized his estimation of her height was off by several inches. This lady was barely a small hand shorter than he was, albeit, 100 pounds lighter.

Mac reached out his ham-sized hand. "I'm Elisias McMaridisch, but most people call me Mac." Her smile and twinkling eyes warmed his heart.

"And I'm Elsha Turnupseed. Most people call me Elsie."

"Are you visiting?" Mac asked.

"Yes, we're staying at the Shilo Inn this week on vacation."

"We?"

"Yes, my parents and I."

"Married?" Mac never confused quiet and shy.

"Not me. My parents are." She flashed a teasing smile. "You?" Elsie blushed a little. Mac couldn't tell which question caused it.

"No. Never met a woman I was willing to put up with." He smiled a little half smile. "Care to ride with me to Willamina tomorrow? I've a couple of loads of logs to deliver to a mill there."

Elsie's eyebrows rose. They too were the color of dry straw and about as distinct against her pale skin as dry beach grass against dry sand. "You're a log truck driver?" She spoke with a tone that would have put any other driver on the defensive.

Mac shrugged and smiled. "Yeah, in part. I raise and harvest my own timber in my own forest. I do all my own repair work, skid my own logs. And I drive my own logs on my own truck to whichever mill pays me the best."

The eyebrows sank back to their normal position. "I think I'd like to," she replied, blushing a tiny bit. "When should I be ready?"

"If you want to make the first run, I'll be by about 6:15 in the morning. If you'd prefer the second run, I'll be by about one."

A pretty smile, Mac thought, as one spread across Elsie's face. "I'll be ready by 6:15 a.m."

"Fine, I'll toot twice on my air horn. The Shilo Inn, correct?"

"That's right."

"Thanks, I'm looking forward to company. I don't have a lot at times."

"Thank you. I've never ridden in a log truck before."

"Good to meet you Elsie. See you tomorrow."

"Yes, see you tomorrow." They shook hands again and Elsie stepped into the center aisle and disappeared out the door. Mac just smiled. Then he remembered, the truck would need to be swamped out. With that, he too headed for the exit. He looked forward to some human company, but he knew his dogs would consider it being gypped out of a ride.

CHAPTER 2

Mac stopped by the grocery store for a few items, among them a box of Constant Comment tea. The clerk teased him about it.

"You're a coffee man, Mac. What's going on?"

Mac chuckled and his cheeks turned pink. "I've got a guest coming for lunch tomorrow. This is supposed to be good tea." Something inside him said to treat this lady well.

At home he greeted his trio of mutts and pitched a couple of Frisbees for them. He gave each one a high-energy scratch/rub from their ears to their rumps.

Inside his log house, he checked his meatloaf and baking potatoes. Just fine. The timer on the oven had worked.

He paused in thought. Lunch tomorrow? It should work out to have it at the house. Steaks! He snapped his fingers as the thought came to him. Two big venison steaks! He turned to his freezer. Ah! He knew just the two. He dug through one shelf until his fingers were bright red. There they were! He'd personally packaged those two. He closed the freezer door and set the package on a plate, finished setting the table for his dinner, served it up, said grace and plowed in.

Dinner completed, he set his cooking pans on the back porch for the dogs to get off the first layer. Mac located his 100-foot extension cord and dragged his 16-gallon Shop-Vac to his truck. In a jerk of awareness, he stopped. Why was he doing this? Vacuuming his not-too-filthy truck to take a stranger for a ride. He glanced at what he hadn't done yet. The dirtiest part of his cab was cleaner than many of his compatriot's trucks at their best. He shrugged and continued cleaning. Somehow this was right.

Monday morning, he fired up his truck and as expected had to defend it against the rush of three dogs wanting to go along. He scratched them all and told them he'd be back for lunch. With a whistle on his lips and a song in his heart, he pulled out for Newport.

———————————

HE PULLED OUT HIS POCKET WATCH AND CHECKED THE TIME— 6:16 a.m. One shot of air and he set the air brakes. Mac tooted his air horn twice as quiet as he could. He waited a moment, then slid out his door and started around his truck, one last check before they really hit the road. Light footsteps behind him caused him to turn. He saw Elsie striding across the street.

They both smiled. Mac reached out a hand like it was the most natural thing in the world. She reached back and they shared a gentle squeeze. "Good morning, Elsie. You're looking refreshed."

"Good morning to you Mac. Thank you. I slept well last night. When will we be back?"

"Five-thirtyish. Why?"

"Father said last night he'd like to meet you. Sometime today we need to stop and call."

"Fine. We can call at lunch." He relaxed his grip so she could pull away. When she didn't, he continued his check, heading for the passenger door.

"What are you doing?" she asked, after he'd tugged a couple cables.

"Just checking my load and my truck. I don't like to lose things on the road."

She chuckled as he opened the passenger side door. Log truck doors are a long way off the ground and not an easy climb for most people. Mac smiled as she gave his hand one more squeeze, released him, gripped the grab irons, put her foot on the narrow step welded to the fuel tank and promptly slipped. Her foot shot off the step and she dangled in the air clutching the grab bars. Mac chuckled. He reached up and tucked one arm behind her knees, his other arm in the small of her back before she lost her grip and fell.

"Let go, I've got you."

Elsie blushed and let go. Mac stepped back with her in his arms, hoping her father wasn't looking. "Thank you," she said, embarrassed.

"That's okay. Mind you, I didn't plan it this way." He smiled at her, as she blushed again and he set her on her feet. He squatted and studied her trousers.

"What are you doing?"

He stood as he replied, "A lot of people who slip like that lose a little skin." He smiled at her and she blushed again. "Just checking." Mac motioned for her to make another try. "Now this time be a little more careful. Take it a little slower, knowing this is your first time in a log truck. Unless, of course, you'd prefer me to just pick you up again and throw you in."

Her pink tinge deepened. "I'll try again, on my own, thanks. Maybe after the fourth time I slip, you can throw me in." Elsie smiled up at him and tried again. He teased her with facetious applause when she settled on the seat. She glared at him with a smile on her lips.

Mac shoved the door closed with a solid thud and walked around to his side. He swung up with a well-practiced grace and ease. "There's three seat belts in here. Take your pick of any—but mine." Elsie blushed as their eyes met. She fished around and found the one on the right end of the big bench seat. She jumped at the spit of compressed air when Mac released the air brakes.

"What a quiet truck," Elsie commented as they got under way. "I always thought big trucks like this made a lot of noise."

"Many do. But I keep this one in pretty good shape. I'm trying harder than usual to keep it quiet too. The powers that be don't like loaded log trucks in this part of town—especially at this hour."

They growled up the hill on Olive and coasted to a stop at the traffic signal on Highway 101. He waved to two other log truck drivers waiting at the light. They gave him questioning looks when they glimpsed Elsie in the cab with him. She gave them a tiny wave and smiled.

Clear of Newport, Mac accelerated and began to point out the sights as the highway wound along on a shelf 60 feet above the edge of the ocean. At the foot of the grade over Cape Foulweather, he downshifted as gravity fought to hold them back. Halfway up he passed another loaded log truck crawling slower than they were. Mac tooted and waved. "That's Gary out of Waldport. He was in the woods about five this morning. That's one reason I like to haul my own logs. I set my own schedule."

By the time they'd reached Willamina, he knew Elsie's father worked as a warden at the federal prison at Sheridan, she'd grown up all over the country and most recently she'd lived in Central California.

AS THEY WAITED IN LINE TO UNLOAD, MAC PULLED OUT HIS thermos. "Like a cup of coffee?" he asked holding it up.

She smiled. "Yes please."

He poured coffee into the lid and handed it to her. "Thanks." She took a sip. "This is good, but aren't you having any?"

"Yes. When you're done. I forgot another cup."

"On purpose, too I'll bet," she teased him.

Mac blushed a little as he pulled forward. "To be honest, no. I just didn't think about another cup. I'm a little mechanical in the morning." He pulled the truck forward again and set the brake. "'Scuse me," he said as he swung out the door.

Elsie watched as Mac released three of the binders that were holding the logs on the truck and stepped back. She wondered why, then gasped when she saw the unloader approaching. The thing looked like a huge yellow tractor with a claw big enough to eat the whole truck in one bite. Mac looked tiny as it moved up to his truck and grabbed the load of eight logs in one big gulp. Mac swung into action again and released the remaining binders.

One wave to the operator and he turned to secure the binders on the truck. As he returned to the cab, Elsie asked in an awed voice, "That thing's what unloads you all the time?"

Mac smiled. "Here, yes. Toledo has some a lot like it. A few mills still have a log pond and use a kind of an A-frame derrick." He pulled forward to a framework with a small electric-powered hoist in the middle. "Excuse me again." With that he was out of the cab, well aware of Elsie watching his every move. Mac lowered the hoist and hooked it onto the rear log bunk. Then he raised the trailer just high enough to clear the front stakes. Scrambling back into the cab, he backed up the truck so the dangling trailer hung poised over the front bunk. Back to the hoist Mac, lowered the trailer. He swung up on the frame of his truck, released the hoist and ran it up out of the way for the next driver.

Back in the cab he grinned at Elsie as he shoved the transmission into gear, "Now, back for load two."

"Would you like to see my house?" Elsie asked before they turned onto the highway back to Mac's place.

Mac glanced at the clock on the dash and shrugged. "Sure, if it's near here."

"Oh, it is. About halfway between here and Sheridan, right on the old road."

"Lead on," he quipped as he pulled to the stop sign at the road.

"Left," she chuckled.

Elsie pointed out her house and Mac slowed, checking it out. Yeah, he could get his empty log truck in the driveway without a major problem.

They rejoined Highway 18 at Sheridan and Mac laid on the fuel for home. He didn't know why knowing where she lived was important, but it somehow was, and he was glad he knew.

As he opened the throttle again south of Newport, Elsie asked, "Now where?"

"Home. First we've got to load the second haul. Then I've got steaks laid out for lunch."

"Steaks?"

"Steak and fried potatoes. Venison steaks to be precise."

"Oh," she responded quietly, like she was considering the menu.

He grinned at her as he braked and downshifted for the left turn off Highway 101 onto Beaver Creek Road. "What's the matter, don't you like venison?"

"I … I don't know. I don't think I've ever had any."

"It's good, I promise. Hang on, I take these curves a little faster than some people like." He whipped his old Kenworth around a series of curves with a smoothness that both appalled and amazed Elsie. He chuckled at her discomfort. "I don't take them like this with a load."

"Good. That would explain why there aren't logs scattered along the side of the road." She flashed him a shy, wan smile.

Five miles in, the road petered out to one graveled lane and he slowed down. Mac reached for his CB. "Mac, inbound empty at the North Beaver Creek bridge." He paused. No response, and he hung up the mike.

"Why'd you do that?" Elsie asked.

"There are others hauling on this road, and I'm rather loathe to be part of a head-on."

"Oh."

Another mile in, they rounded one more curve and he slowed, as they topped a rise. "There's home," he told her, pointing to a small log house across the narrow valley.

"Oh, I love it." The log house sat on a shoulder of the hill, looking out at a 180-degree view of the valley. A porch spread across the entire front side. The shallow pitched shake roof rose from the edge of the porch in a straight line to the ridge centered on the house. A tall, river-rock chimney covered much of one end.

Behind the house stood a two-story, log, barn-like structure. Between them and the house was a half-mile wide green, grassy field with four-foot wide Beaver Creek wandering between pasture and road. A half dozen cows and two horses grazed, not even looking up. Mac paused on the road. "I'll show you the inside after we get loaded." He released the clutch and guided the truck over a bridge that in a former life was a Union Pacific Railroad flat car, past the house and up a narrow dirt road. As he passed the house, his three dogs burst out of their daytime hiding places and stood in silence, tails slack, begging for a ride with their eyes.

As they wound deeper into the woods, Elsie rolled down her window and sighed. "It's beautiful up here, Mac. How much of this is yours?"

"The watershed of this valley. Officially, it's 352 acres, about 90 percent of it is forest." He slowed the truck to a crawl. "Look." Mac pointed to a doe and two yearling fawns on the road in front of them.

"Oh! They're beautiful!" Elsie exclaimed.

"Out here, yes. Those three don't venture down near the house much, so they're not on my blacklist."

"Your blacklist?" She gave him a blank look.

"Yes. The only deer I harvest are those who help themselves to my garden."

She looked at him in shock, then began laughing. "And I suppose you have them named too."

"No," he replied chuckling, "I just figure if I feed them, they can feed me."

The road widened and they crawled past a stack of a couple dozen logs. "About six of those are our load."

"Where are we going?" Elsie asked as they continued on.

"To turn around. I've got another landing around the corner that's clear."

The road widened again, and Mac backed the truck around. In two tries, he had them heading downhill again. He gave her a sheepish smile. "I usually do that in one move. Somehow it wasn't worth it today."

"Thanks. We were very close to the edge."

"That's just the perspective from the cab. I doubt we were closer than 10 feet from any edge."

"Oh."

Mac stopped the Kenworth just short of the stack of logs. Elsie jumped again at the spurt of compressed air when Mac set the air brakes. He turned to her. "Most of my work at this stop is from the loader." He motioned to the crane-like apparatus with a claw behind the cab. "You can stay in the cab and watch if you wish. Or watch from the ground."

"I'd like to get out for a while, if you don't mind."

"No. Just stay on the road, uphill of the truck please."

"Okay." Mac swung down and was climbing toward his seat on the loader by the time Elsie had—one step at a time—lowered herself to the ground. Mac smiled and waved, as she walked past the truck. He motioned her to continue when she stopped too close to where he'd be working.

When he was satisfied that she was safely out of the way, he grabbed the trailer with the loader and set it on the ground. Back into the cab, he set the trailer brakes and pulled ahead, stretching the truck out to the right length for this load. He saw Elsie smile at him as he swung up to the seat on the loader. He smiled back and turned to his task. One log at a time, he loaded the trailer. Bunks full, he checked the scales built into the rig. He pushed a couple logs back to balance the load, checked the scales again, tucked the loader into its storage position and climbed down. On the ground he threw the required binders around the load and snugged them down. He dusted his hands, turned and walked toward Elsie.

"That was quick and efficient," she commented as he came near.

"Thank you. On a typical day, I'm out here alone and just do the job as quick as I can. Come, let's walk a minute." He reached a hand toward her and she reached back.

Hand in hand, they wandered to the landing where he'd turned around. There they looked south over the valley to tree-covered hill after hill fading into purple through the haze. He pointed west. "That's the ocean. At least on a clear day you can see it."

"Mac. It's beautiful out here. So quiet." She turned to him with a contented smile on her face. "Thank you for inviting me."

"It is indeed my pleasure. I don't often have company of your quality. Come, my stomach tells me it's near lunch time." Together they turned and started back to the truck.

Just before they got back to the truck, Elsie stopped. "What's that smell?" She wrinkled her nose.

Mac stopped beside her and shrugged. "I don't know. I've tried to track it, but I've never found the source."

"Oh." She paused and smiled up at him. "And if it's a skunk, you're better off not finding it." They both laughed.

This time he boosted her through his door. "There, was that easier?" he asked as he climbed in.

"Yes. You seem to know how to do that."

Mac grinned at her. "Oh yes, my nieces and nephews love to ride with me when they're here. All of them have been too small to even reach the first grab." They both chuckled as Mac put the truck in gear and released the brake. It growled back down the hill to the house.

CHAPTER 3

When Elsie stepped in the front door, she gasped and stopped cold. He glanced around the room and saw it from her perspective. To their right, the river-rock fireplace, with its glass door insert, took up most of the wall at the end of the room. A slate hearth formed a six-foot semicircle in front of the fireplace. Covering the floor in front of the furniture was a genuine bearskin rug—complete with head and toothy grin. A brown-and-cream plaid lounge sat under the front windows, two high-backed comfortable chairs faced the fireplace and a love seat backed up to a seven-foot-tall doorway in the wall that ran down the center of the house. To the left was a large, round dining table. The polished wood floor reflected two skylights over the dining area.

The left end of the wall opened to a compact kitchen. Two bedrooms and a bath opened off the living area. Between the tall doors, bookcases rose from the floor to the loft, comfortably full of many sizes of books.

"I like it," Elsie gasped. "It's so homey and appropriate for here."

"Thank you. I designed and built it. Though my sister and sister-in-law helped design the kitchen. Come, I need to start lunch." They shared a smile.

"I need to use the bathroom first. I'll be right out." She hurried to the appropriate door as Mac headed to the kitchen. The grill and griddle smelled well on the way to ready when Elsie stepped to the counter. "May I help?" she asked, smiling as she settled on one of the stools at the breakfast counter.

"Sure, if you're willing to peel or grate potatoes."

"Pass me the peeler." Within minutes they had the griddle covered with steaming potatoes and the two steaks on the grill.

"Come, I'll show you around." The door nearest the fireplace was the guest room, where a queen bed with a handmade quilt on it sat off to the right of the door with a small dresser under the window.

They stepped through the middle door, his bedroom.

"Isn't that a king-sized bed?" Elsie asked.

"Yes, a California king. I love it. It almost fits me," he responded with a chuckle.

She blushed when he looked at her.

They shared a smile, then scurried to the kitchen to finish preparing lunch.

"Oh, I need to call the motel to tell Father when he can expect us. Do you mind if he takes you out to dinner?"

"Only if you're not around." Mac grinned at her.

"I assume Mother and I are included," she smiled back at him and ducked her head just a little. "What time can I tell him?"

"Tell him six tonight."

"Thanks."

Mac set lunch on the table as Elsie hung up the phone. "It's okay by him."

"Good. Let's eat."

———

AT FIVE THAT AFTERNOON, MAC PULLED OFF HIGHWAY 101 NEAR the crest of Cape Foulweather. He pulled into the parking lot at the overlook. "Have you ever stopped here?" he asked.

The parking lot sat on top of a massive outcropping of rock, nearly a thousand feet above the ocean. A four-foot-high chain link fence surrounded the parking lot, marking the upper edge of the nearly vertical drop to the waves. A path between the fence and the edge of the parking area led out to a narrow fence-lined promontory.

"No, I haven't! Can we check it out?" she responded with the enthusiasm of a child wanting to go explore.

"Sure. Let me park this rig." Moments later they walked hand in hand just inside the fence. Out on the point Mac pointed out the Yaquina Head Lighthouse, the Yaquina River jetties.

"You like living at the beach don't you," Elsie observed.

"Yes, I do. I wouldn't live anywhere else. And living where I do, I have the best of both worlds. Away from the ocean, it's warmer, and the winds are blunted a little." He glanced at his watch. "Come, it's time to get rolling."

With one long look at the ocean far below them and the rocks offshore, she reached for his hand and walked with him back to the truck. "Would you like to make a run into Eugene with me on Friday? I have to deliver a couple loads of cedar, and my first haul is Friday."

"One or two trips?"

"One. It's just too long a trip to make two worth my time. Some guys make two, but usually not me."

"I'd love to."

"Thanks. It's a pleasure to have you along. We'll be going south along Cape Perpetua and Heceta Head. It's beautiful country."

"Same time?"

Mac paused. "Yes. That way I'm out of this area before the tourist traffic begins to build."

The nearest parking space for his rig turned out to be a block and a half away from the Shilo Inn and it was 6 p.m. on the dot as they walked up to the entrance. The couple Mac recognized as those with Elsie Sunday morning stepped from under the awning.

Elsie butchered and stumbled over Mac's last name. Mac just smiled. "That's why most everyone calls me Mac."

Elsie introduced her father George and mother, Fran. George scrutinized Mac's jeans, flannel shirt and suspenders. "Where's a good place to eat, Eliss … Elizar … ah, Mac." The pale man blushed as he stumbled over Mac's first name.

"The Flagship is fine," Mac responded with a chuckle.

"Good. Now where is it?"

"Right here," Mac replied, chuckling, motioning to the restaurant beside them.

George startled as Mac held the door open for all of them. As they waited for their dinners, a middle-aged, professorial-looking man in a business suit strolled over to their table. He looked Mac in the eye.

"You drive that old self-loader out there?" He made it sound like an accusation.

Mac met his eyes. "The forest green one down the street?"

"Yeah, that one." The man ranted on about how "gypo" loggers cut and run, and their trucks aren't safe.

Mac cut him off, when he had to take a breath. "You sound like you know a lot about the woods and such."

"That's right."

Mac interrupted again. "Do you recall who was Oregon tree farmer of the year three years ago?"

The man straightened and wrinkled his forehead in thought. "Somebody called Elijah McMartinish or something like that. He lives on the coast somewhere."

Mac stood, looked down at the man and extended his hand. "Pleased to meet you. I'm Elisias McMaridisch. You know about my tree farming. Talk to any other legitimate logger in the county about my truck. I've been offered enough to buy a brand new one, cash." The man paled in part because of the revelation of who Elisias was and in part because of the crushing grip Mac had on his hand. Mac smiled and released the man's hand. "Have a good day."

The man scurried away shaking his right hand and Mac settled back in his chair. Elsie grinned at him. Mac winked back. "You certainly handled that well," George commented.

"Thanks. There are some around who think us independent loggers are a cheap bunch. Granted, there are some who work for the buck and nothing else. But most of us love the woods and take care of our equipment. I'm sure there are both kinds in your field too."

George nodded, acknowledging the wisdom of Mac's statement. Dinner arrived and conversation continued. Mac talked about his place, George and Fran talked about their life together. Elsie chuckled as Mac finished her large helping of prawns when she stalled out.

"Oh," Mac spoke up. "Why don't you come out for dinner Wednesday night. All of you. Elsie, do you think you can find the place now?"

Elsie nodded.

"Good. I've also asked Elsie to ride to Eugene with me Friday. I'll need to pick her up about the same time, and she'll be back before six again."

Her parents nodded.

"Good. Thank you for dinner." All four stood and Mac reached across the table and shook George's hand. Mac rested one huge hand on Fran's shoulder. "It's good to meet all of you." He turned to Elsie. "I've enjoyed today. Thanks for coming. I'll see all of you about six for dinner. I'll be busy during the day, so please don't come too early. We'll have lots of time afterwards to see the place." He nodded to each one and they left the restaurant.

Outside, Fran laid her skinny hand on Mac's thick arm. "Thank you for coming. We'll be there Wednesday evening."

Mac squeezed her hand. "Thank you. I'm looking forward to it." He turned to Elsie. "Good night, Elsie. I'll see you Wednesday, too."

Another nod, and he strode to his log truck. He waved as he pulled past the trio. He stopped at South Beach Fish Market in South Beach, for two orders of fish and chips with a large Pepsi to fill in the cracks left unfilled from dinner.

Little did he know the other female would push his Wednesday night dinner plans.

CHAPTER 4

Tuesday, Mac swept and dusted his house, harvested and froze 10 quarts of broccoli and cauliflower from his garden, then cleaned up his kitchen. He refueled and washed both trucks. As he worked, he mused about Wednesday's dinner menu. Ah! Salmon! Mac turned to his freezer and removed a middle-sized silver. That would do. He dug out a serving tray, slipped it under the foil wrapped fish and slid them all into the refrigerator.

Wednesday morning, Mac saddled one of his horses and headed for the woods. The dogs followed with tails whipping, racing this way and that until he headed up the road. As they traveled farther into the woods, he guided the horse to the road he preferred to use to get at his cedar tomorrow. That road had a couple of soft places and one area prone to rockslides.

Something about the woods made him relish rides like this. On horseback he seemed to be able to get closer to the creatures of the wild. He regularly glimpsed deer, bear and, a couple of times, a cougar.

At each soft place in the road, he swung off the horse, inspected the drain tiles and general condition of the road. When he headed the horse on up the road after his last check, he said a little prayer of thanks. The truck would make it through, even loaded.

At the curve before the rockslide, the dogs froze, let out one terrified yelp and tails between their legs, bolted back down the road. A moment later, Mac heard a scrambling from out of sight. A scrambling of several large animals, a guttural near growl, then the ominous sound of a rockslide. Without warning, the horse bolted, and Mac found himself on his back in the ditch.

Dazed, he shook his head, rolled over, rocked to his knees and struggled to his feet, grateful he'd been thrown on the uphill side of the road. A clatter of a falling rock brought his mind back to his errand. The wind brought a whiff of the odor he and Elsie had smelled on the landing overlooking the valley.

When he rounded the corner, he sighed in relief. The slide hadn't blocked the road. But a second glance brought him up short. In the ditch, both legs pinned under the edge of the slide lay an ape-like creature. It lay still, unconscious. As Mac approached with even more caution than meeting a bear or cougar, the odor grew stronger. Now he knew what it was. A sasquatch! A bigfoot! He estimated this one was a little over six feet tall, covered with three- to four-inch long black to brown hair resembling a gorilla but different. It didn't move as he approached in hunting mode.

The rattle of another rock drew his attention away from the creature. This slide looked extremely unstable. He'd almost lost his D-4 trying to clear one away a couple years ago. He took another glance at the sasquatch. If that slide let loose again, it would bury the creature. He couldn't let that happen. Mac strode to where a half dozen rocks pinned its legs. None of them too big for Mac to move.

He started in, one rock at a time. The odor grew stronger and he glanced up. Another sasquatch was working beside him. They stopped a moment and sized each other up. Mac looked up and met its eyes. Wow! This creature was tall! This sasquatch looked older. Black to brown hair covered it, with a sprinkling of gray hairs on its head and chest.

A second later they both bent to the task of clearing the slide. This creature was strong. Mac realized that when it picked up a rock he'd have struggled with. Together they hefted a small boulder and pitched it out of the way.

Within minutes, they freed the smaller sasquatch's legs. The larger one grunted what could only have been a thank you, scooped up the other one as someone would pick up an injured child, scrambled up the bank and disappeared into the woods.

Mac stood gazing at where the two had vanished. Vanished like a deer. Only unlike a deer, the strange acrid odor remained. It had happened. He glanced at the ditch at his feet. There in the soft dirt remained a human shaped imprint. He paused only a moment, then began clearing the road, pitching the rocks to cover the evidence.

Road cleared, he glanced up where the slide had come from. At the top, he thought he saw a shadow leap out of sight. He blinked, but nothing changed. Mac refocused on the slide itself. It was safe for the time being. He could get his truck up the road for his loads. He glanced at the shadows the trees threw across the road. Then he whipped out his pocket watch—2:30 p.m.! No wonder he was hungry! He headed back down the road, calculating in his head how long it would take to get dinner on the table after the long walk back to his house. Time to hurry! His long strides took him down the road at a pace that would have forced a more typical sized person to at least jog to keep abreast.

When he got home, there was his horse, grazing near the barn. What a welcome sight. He headed in his direction.

———————

A SHORT TIME LATER, JUST AS HE WAS SETTING A PLATE FULL OF cheese-sauce-covered, fresh cauliflower in the microwave, his dogs started a ruckus. He bent and glanced through the front windows. A silvery-gray, mid-sized car was just crossing the bridge. Mac had long ago given up on new car identification. He looked again. Three people inside. Elsie and her parents. A smile crossed his face as he turned and checked the salmon in the oven. Virtually done. Good. He hung his denim apron on its peg and hurried to the front door. He called his dogs to order and greeted his guests.

A firm handshake for George, a gentle hug around the shoulders for Fran and Elsie. They stopped on the porch and surveyed the view before them. A kingfisher flashed into the creek and came up with a fish just as a sigh escaped from Elsie, standing beside him.

"You picked a dandy location," George commented, respecting the quiet around them.

"Thank you. I like it here," Mac replied without conceit. "Come in. Dinner is just about ready."

Mac held the door for the three of them. Fran gasped and stopped as she stepped in. "Mac! I didn't believe Elsie when she described your place. Even her most glowing attributes don't do it justice. What a delightful house!"

"Thank you. May I take your coats?" he asked with a slight bow. Elsie and her parents slipped off their jackets, and he laid them on his guest bed. "Excuse me, but I have a few finishing touches on dinner. Elsie, come help please." Elsie followed without any hesitation.

His guests exclaimed at the scents of dinner. Fran settled on a stool at his breakfast counter. George perused the bookshelves and Mac kept Elsie busy carrying things to the table.

After grace, they joined in a delightful meal. George and Fran kept complimenting his cooking, and Mac smiled, accepting their compliments. His earlier incident in the woods slipped into the back of his mind.

After dinner, Elsie and Fran headed for the kitchen. Mac shooed them both out. "I'll just stack the dishes and be right with you."

Fran protested a little but departed for the living room without further encouragement. Elsie turned and Mac gave her a reassuring smile at her tiny hurt look. He stepped to her, laid his huge hands on her shoulders and met her eyes. "Elsie, today you are a guest in this house. I will not deny the possibility that may change, but today you are a guest. I'll be out in a minute." She smiled, he pivoted her and gave her a gentle push out of the kitchen.

George looked up from his squatting position in front of the bookcase as Mac stepped back into his living area. "This is quite a collection. Everything from serious to sublime to ridiculous." Fran shot him a dirty look. "A lot of children's books, considering you don't have any."

Mac grinned and chuckled. "My sister and brother both have three apiece. They all come a couple times a year. When they come in the winter, one of the favorite pastimes is curling up on that bear rug and reading in front of the fire."

George straightened. "You read to them?"

Mac shrugged. "Sometimes. Mostly I tell stories of the woods."

"What do you do for entertainment? I don't see a television or stereo."

"Entertainment?" Mac looked buffaloed a moment. "Oh! How do I keep busy?" He chuckled. "It isn't difficult. Yesterday, I froze about 20 pounds of broccoli and cauliflower out of my garden. This morning, I rode one of my horses up to check out the road I have to take tomorrow to get my load of cedar for Friday." He paused a moment as he thought better of mentioning his adventure with the sasquatch. Only Elsie caught his slight blush and hesitation. "In the fall I hunt. When the weather's too bad to log, I work on my truck and buildings. I read a lot in the evenings. My stereo is tucked away at the end of the bookcase." He motioned in that direction. "I don't like television and can't get anything out here anyway." He chuckled. "Typically, one weekend in March or April, we have a church wood-cutting party out here."

"Wood-cutting party?" George raised his eyebrows.

"Yes. I get together with two or three other loggers in the church, and we haul a couple loads of mostly alder down here to the flat. Then anyone who wants wood comes and helps cut. The younger men tend to run the chain saw, while the rest of us chuckle at their posturing. We also split, stack and load the wood. Most of the ladies herd kids or help in the kitchen. It's a lot of fun, plus it keeps several families warm in the winter." Mac motioned to the chairs. "Sit and chat a minute?"

George shook his head. "In a minute maybe. I'd like to see the rest of your place with just you." He met Mac's eyes in almost a challenge. Mac glanced at Elsie. Elsie rolled her eyes, like she knew what was coming.

Mac shrugged. Elsie's reaction made him think maybe he did too. "Sure, come on." He fetched George's coat and handed it to him. Together the men walked out the door. As they crossed in front of the porch he noticed Elsie and her mother head for the kitchen. Halfway to his barn/shop, Mac asked, "What would you like to see, buildings or critters?"

"Mostly, I wanted to talk to you alone," George responded in all seriousness. A less confident man would have heard a threat in his words.

"Why?" Mac responded, feigning innocence.

"What are your designs on my daughter?"

"Elsie? None right now. I intend to court her for a reasonable length of time to get to know her better. She seems a delightful young lady."

George eyed Mac a moment. "Treat her well. I insist that the first time you take her to your bed is your wedding night."

A smile crawled across Mac's face. " I can live with your request. Now what is her dowry?" Mac couldn't help but tease the lanky, smaller man beside him.

George startled, blanched and looked down at his shoes. "I … I'm not sure I know what you mean."

Mac laughed and gave George a mild punch on his shoulder. "Don't worry about it. I haul into Willamina now and then, and I expect to be able to stop in and see her. I hope you don't mind a log truck in your drive once in a while."

George looked up at him. "No … no, I don't mind. I've learned some people don't like independent loggers. What kind of tag do you hang on yourself?"

Mac rumbled a chuckle. "Depends on who I'm trying to impress. The IRS thinks I'm a forest products entrepreneur. I'm a log truck driver to most of the kids, a tree farmer to the extension service. To most of the people at church I'm a gentle, lovable, honorable giant."

George chuckled. "I see," he responded as he looked up into Mac's eyes. "I can accept that. And few people ever question any of them."

"Never after they meet me face-to-face." Both men laughed.

George extended his hand. "I'm pleased to make your acquaintance."

Mac engulfed the man's hand in his own. "Thank you. Let's go get the ladies and show them around too."

Darkness brought the tour to a close. As Mac escorted Elsie and her family back to their car, Elsie hung back a moment. Mac stopped next to her. "Something happen in the woods today?" she asked in a near whisper.

"Yes," he replied, smiling at the memory, meeting her eyes. "Nothing dangerous or risky. We'll talk about it Friday."

"Okay. See you about 6:15 a.m."

"I'm looking forward to it."

He opened a back door of the car and she slid into the seat. Goodbyes were repeated, and they were gone in the dust and dusk. Mac smiled to himself as he wandered back to his house. He could wait for her. Just the same, he looked forward to getting to know her better.

CHAPTER 5

riday morning, Mac pulled up in front of the Shilo Inn. He set the brakes and reached for the air horn cord. Before he could give it a gentle tug, he looked up and smiled as Elsie walked toward him. He climbed out of the truck and greeted her with an outstretched hand.

She took his hand, and they shared a smile.

"Good morning Elsie. Did you go out and buy the jeans and flannel shirt?" He couldn't help but tease her, dressed much as he was, sans suspenders.

Elsie blushed. "The shirt, yes. Do you approve?"

"If you're trying to be comfortable at the beach, yes. If you're trying to simply look like a logger without being willing to be one, no."

"Oh?" Her eyebrows rose as they walked hand in hand around the truck.

At the right-side door, she climbed in without a hitch.

"Been practicing?" Mac teased.

"Only on your truck." She smiled and winked at him.

As Mac cleared the Newport city limits southbound and accelerated to the speed limit, he asked, "Did I pass inspection Wednesday?"

Elsie smiled and chuckled. "Oh, yes. Mother was very impressed with your place. And your cooking." She turned and gave him a sly glance. "And Father says I have permission to allow you to court me."

A light laugh escaped Mac. "Not that he could do much about it."

"No, I suppose not. But since I'm still living at home, he does have a certain right to screen who he lets in his house."

"I suppose. Why do you still live at home?"

"Mac," Elsie replied, "that's a story for later. Suffice it to say, I prefer it at this point in my life."

"I can accept that." He downshifted for the wide horseshoe curve at Beaver Creek and Brian Booth State Park. Around the corner and over a small rise, Mac picked up speed again, then slowed as they approached the small community of Seal Rock.

There the road shouldered up to the ocean breaking on the rocks 100 feet offshore. He pulled into what was signed a slow vehicle turnout.

He edged the truck near the guardrail, stopped and set the brakes. "Quite a sight isn't it? The waves breaking on those rocks."

"Oh, it is!" Elsie exclaimed, enthralled. She kept her eyes on the waves crashing over the basalt rocks standing in the way of the breakers. She turned from the window and met Mac's eyes. "I'm not used to the perspective from a truck. You sit so high up."

Mac grinned back. "That's one reason I like them. Let's keep moving." He glanced in his mirror, paused for a lone pickup to clear, released the brake and checked his mirrors again. A light-colored Lincoln pulled in the overlook behind him, and he pulled out.

Mac downshifted as he started down the grade at the north end of the Alsea Bay bridge. "There's good reason for the speed limit on this bridge, there's quite a downgrade on the other end."

Clear of Waldport, Mac accelerated again. "I prefer to drive this route early in the morning. There's so much less traffic, especially in the summer." Yachats fell behind them, and they started up and around the face of Cape Perpetua. Here the mountains marched into the sea. The nearly vertical basalt cliffs rose 300 feet from the roaring breakers to a narrow shelf, cut for the road. The cliff continued up and up on the other side of the road. Elsie edged away from the window.

"Mac! It's beautiful! But the road's so narrow! And so close to the cliff!"

Mac chuckled and glanced in his wide mirrors. "Oh, I've got a foot to the center line and two feet to the right edge." He slowed and pulled into a viewpoint large enough for his truck, partly to let Elsie look, and partly to let a cream-colored Lincoln pass. The Lincoln rounded the curve and disappeared.

Mac pointed out Heceta Head in the hazy distance. Elsie ooh'd and ah'd over it all. "I've never seen anything like this! Thank you for bringing me!" She turned and smiled at him.

"You're most welcome, but let's keep moving."

Another loaded log truck growled by, and Mac and the driver shared a toot on their air horns.

As they passed, Mac pointed out the road leading to Cape Perpetua Visitor Center. At the straight stretch south of Cape Perpetua just before Ten Mile Creek, Mac slowed to let the Lincoln pass. It didn't. "Last chance for him for a while," Mac muttered.

"What?" Elsie turned from watching the ocean.

"Oh, I've had a fancy car on my tail since Seal Rock. It went by us at the viewpoint before the visitor center, but it's behind us again. I slowed down a bit ago to let him pass." Mac shrugged.

"Maybe he doesn't want to," Elsie commented with a quiet, serious tone.

Mac glanced at her. "Why wouldn't someone want to pass a loaded log truck on this road?" he responded out of surprise.

"That I can't answer. I do know Father has had people follow him for various and disgusting reasons."

"Oh." They rode on in silence a moment as Mac downshifted and braked preparing for the hairpin turn on the south flank of Heceta Head. He glanced in his mirror. The Lincoln was still there. "Should I stop and confront him?"

Elsie shook her head. "No, not now. Father always says that's dangerous. You don't know what he wants or what he has with him. Find reinforcements first."

A sly smile spread over Mac's face. "I hadn't ever thought about it before, but you're wise. Lord knows what he's after. I'll give him one more chance to pass me. If he doesn't, I'll call in reinforcements like you've never seen."

They wound past Sea Lion Caves and the curves beyond. Mac slowed and pulled off at a viewpoint just big enough for the truck. The Lincoln slipped past them. "I've got the license number," Elsie told him in a quiet, no-nonsense voice.

"Thanks. Let's go." Again, they moved back onto the highway.

Two pull off's later, they rolled past the Lincoln. Three curves later, Mac caught sight of it in his mirrors. "Still there," he grumbled. The smile came back, and he reached for his CB mike. He winked at Elsie. "Here goes."

He squeezed the mike button and spoke. "This is Mac. I'm north of Florence, headed for Eugene with a load of shake logs, and I've got somebody following me. I'd like to meet a couple of you log truck drivers somewhere convenient, so we can find out what he's up to. Mac out."

Silence a moment. Then the radio crackled. "Mac, what's your twenty?"

"Twenty?" Elsie asked, a blank look on her face.

"Location," Mac replied. He turned his attention to the microphone. "South bound on 101, just passed C&M Stables."

"10-4, meet us in the yard at Davidson."

"10-4. Be there in about 30 minutes."

"Us?" Elsie queried, her eyebrows shooting upward.

Mac chuckled. "Yes, us. There'll be at least three other trucks plus yard workers. They know me at that mill."

"Good," Elsie sighed in relief.

Mac chuckled again when the radio crackled. "Mac, is a cream Lincoln the rig following you?"

"10-4."

"What was that all about?" Elsie asked.

Mac pointed to a loaded log truck and an empty chip truck idling along the main drag leading into Florence. "That's the truck that went around us on the face of Cape Perpetua. Watch, they'll probably pull out behind us."

They both watched the mirrors and shortly the Lincoln was not so subtly sandwiched between Mac and the second log truck. The chipper brought up the rear.

At the left turn off 101 onto Highway 126 in downtown Florence, Mac motioned two more log trucks on in front of him. A third one motioned him on.

The parade cleared the city limits, Mac glanced in his mirror and chuckled. "Check your mirror, Elsie. This is quite a convoy."

Elsie looked. "Yes, but how many are in it?"

"Including us, five loaded log trucks, one empty chip truck and a state patrol car."

"A state patrol car?" Elsie exclaimed.

Mac nodded. "The trooper joined us as we passed their office in Florence." He reached for his CB. "This is Mac. I don't know what kind of reception is planned, but let's at least give our guest an honest chance to explain himself."

A chorus of 10-4's crackled back.

The driver of the Lincoln tried to slip out of line, but a battered pickup sporting a variety of antennas boxed him in. The parade pulled into the mill yard intact.

A square built logger familiar to Mac waved the parade down an aisle between two lines of other loaded log trucks. As he set his brake, he glanced in his mirrors. The Lincoln was directly behind him, the three trucks following him were directed to the end of the other lines. The patrol car stopped behind the Lincoln. Ten truck drivers, at least that many mill workers and two Oregon State patrolmen approached the Lincoln.

The man at the wheel turned pale and rolled down his window. He paled further when he really looked around him.

Mac stepped over to his window. "Come on out, we're not out to harm you. We just want to know why you were following me."

The door eased open and the man slid out of his seat. He could have been another truck driver, six feet or so tall, tolerably muscled. He extended a quivering hand to Mac. "I'm Sam Pentice. I'm a log buyer. I saw your load this morning and wanted to find out where you got it, so I could buy some.

There's not a lot of cedar of that quality coming out of the woods these days."

Mac smiled and relieved chuckles rose around the car. Mac enclosed the man's hand in his own. "Most folks call me Mac. You know good timber when you see it, but all my cedar is sold for the rest of the year."

Sam's face fell. "Damn. I'm willing to pay good money for timber like that. What are you getting for that load?"

Mac told him and Sam's jaw fell open. Startled gasps came from the men around them. "I'm willing to offer you five times that! I could write you a check for that load and as many more you care to deliver."

Mac eyed the smaller man a long moment, furrows growing in his forehead. "If I sold you some timber, what would you do with it?" he asked, suspicious even though he felt he knew.

"I have orders for as much cedar as I can get my hands on at almost any price for log buyers in Japan."

The atmosphere in that mill yard grew tense. "Mr. Pentice, first, all of my cedar cutting is sold for this year. The reason I sold it for that price is the mill I'm delivering it to was about to go out of business because they couldn't get any logs at a reasonable price. Second, NONE of my logs go outside this country before they've been worked on here." Mac's voice took on a tone of quiet rage, and he stepped threateningly toward Sam. "Don't ever come looking for me, if you've any thought of selling them overseas. Do you understand?"

Sam took a quick step behind his car door. He paled, then sputtered, "You're missing a pretty fabulous offer. You could buy a new truck."

"I have guaranteed three loads of cedar, and I will deliver on time and on price. I also don't take jobs away from American men. And don't insult my truck. Most of the men here have cast envious eyes on it." An angry murmur rose from the assembled men.

Sam cast a nervous glance around the circle. "And I'll make the same offer to any of you."

All of the truck drivers and most of the mill workers in the circle shook their heads. Mac turned to the patrolmen. "Officer, could you move your vehicle so Sam can leave?"

The officer grinned, strode to his patrol car, and backed it out of the way. Sam got in his car, gunned the engine in reverse and sped out of the yard in a cloud of dust, flying gravel and squealing tires.

The men gathered around Mac and slapped him on his back hard enough that a typical man would have stumbled forward. "Mac, you had us wondering, thought maybe you had a hijacker on your tail!"

Mac grinned. "You might say I did." They all laughed deep and long. Laughter lessening, Mac roared above the crowd. "I thank you all, my treat for coffee next door."

The men laughed again. "Mac, you know it's not break time. We gotta get to work!"

"Well, then if any of you catch me in a cafe, your coffee's on me." Cheers. Mac laughed with them. "Thank you all. I owe you all a favor."

Someone called, "All right, Mac. We want to meet the lady."

Mac turned to Elsie. He chuckled to himself as he stepped over to her, standing next to a patrolman. Her pink shade was not sunburn. "I'd like you to meet Elsie." He looped one long arm around her shoulder and looked around the circle of men. "Elsie Turnupseed. She's new in the area and never ridden in a log truck." He grinned. "Her father has given me permission to court her, but that's all." Elsie blushed as scattered whistles and applause rose from the circle.

Several of the men greeted her as the others found their way back to the mill or their trucks.

The officers stepped up to Mac and smiled. Mac extended his big hand. "Thank you, gentlemen. We didn't even call you."

"No, but we monitor the CB and heard the call. Thought we'd better check it out. It could have been serious."

Mac nodded. "I doubt I'll see Sam Pentice again for a while."

"Probably not. See you later, Mac."

The officers shook hands with Elsie. "Does your father work at Sheridan?"

Elsie nodded, surprised that an officer in Oregon would know her father.

"I worked with him in California a couple years. Good man. I'm pleased to meet you, Elsie."

"Thank you," Elsie responded. "It's good to meet you."

Handshakes around again, and the patrolmen climbed into their car, waved and drove off.

Mac reached for Elsie's hand, and she reached back. They shared a smile. "That didn't turn out too bad. Not near as exciting as in the movies."

Elsie chuckled. "It's just fine with me." Her voice turned serious. "One of Father's co-workers was killed when he confronted a man following him."

"Thank you for your wisdom." He laid both hands on her shoulder so she couldn't climb back in his truck. As he turned her around their eyes met. "May I kiss you?"

Elsie blushed. "I guess so," she whispered.

The kiss was gentle but burned with a promise of more. Elsie pulled away when a chorus of cheers and catcalls erupted behind them. Faster than she ever had before, she climbed into the truck.

Mac waved to his laughing harassers as he walked around the rear of the truck, checking his load. He swung up into the cab, grinned at Elsie, released the brake and murmured, "Let's get moving."

CHAPTER 6

Mac maneuvered the truck out of the yard at Mapleton back onto the highway to Eugene. They waved and smiled at many of the men working there. Even Mac's truck struggled with the long grade eastbound toward the Petersen Tunnel through Mapleton Hill. Halfway up they caught up with a truck Elsie recognized as one that had been at the mill. Mac downshifted twice and crawled up the hill 50 yards behind.

"Why don't you go around him?" Elsie asked, breaking the silence.

"Because I'm not going enough faster, and there isn't a passing lane. Besides, that driver makes the best time he can wherever he goes. He's got his foot to the floor now and will hold it there even on the downhill side." Mac chuckled. "He's left more than one load on the side of the road. No, I'd just slow him up on the downhill side. I'm not in that much of a hurry." He glanced over at Elsie and smiled. She smiled back.

Clear of the tunnel, Mac asked, just loud enough to be heard over the engine, "Elsie, do you believe in the existence of sasquatch? Bigfoot?"

Elsie gave him a forehead-furrowed look. After a long moment, she spoke with a suspicious tone in her voice. "I'm not sure. There have been rumors of a lot of sightings by rational people. But ... " Her voice trailed off.

"Am I a rational person, Elsie?"

Her straw-colored eyebrows rose toward her hairline. Silence save for the whistle of the slip stream around the truck, the whine of the tires and the low rumble of the engine. The eyebrows settled back into place, then moved together as she eyed Mac with suspicious scrutiny. "So far I have found you very rational. At times a little peculiar, but very rational."

Mac took a deep breath. "You asked me Wednesday night if something had happened in the woods that day."

"Yes." She gave him a noncommittal response.

"That something was a sasquatch." He paused. "Actually, not one sasquatch but two and possibly a third." He glanced at Elsie. She still sat watching him, her eyebrows close together, forehead furrowed. Mac smiled. "You don't believe me, do you?"

Her forehead relaxed and her eyebrows returned to their normal position. "Tell me about it."

"Well," Mac began. He unwound the story of meeting the creature and the larger one helping out. "But Elsie, it spoke to me," Mac told her when he finished.

"Spoke to you?"

"Yes. Oh, I didn't understand the sounds it made, but as the larger one scooped up the smaller one, it said thank you."

Their eyes met. "Then they're really intelligent creatures, not just North American escaped gorillas."

Mac nodded as he downshifted for the light at Veneta. "I have to think so. And the way he picked up the one that had been pinned by the slide. It was like a father picking up his child."

They rode in silence until Mac pulled into the industrial section of west Eugene. "Oh, Elsie?"

"Yes, Mac?"

"This needs to be kept absolutely silent. If any word gets out, my place will be trampled by curiosity seekers. I don't want that."

"I understand."

"I mean silence even to your parents, friends. Everyone."

Elsie opened her mouth to say something, then paused. "Yes, Mac. Complete silence. I would hate to think what would happen if the word ever got out."

"Thank you, Elsie." He pointed toward a cluster of silver-colored, corrugated-metal buildings surrounded by a tall cyclone fence.

"That's where we're headed."

As they pulled into the mill yard, Mac commented. "See, they don't have a lot of timber left. My three loads will help out a great deal."

Elsie looked around. No, there weren't a lot of logs around, especially after the mill at Mapleton. A man waved and directed them to pull next to a small cold deck about the size of three truck loads. Mac set the brake. "Stay put a minute, Elsie. I need to find out what he wants done with my load." He swung out of the cab. The man walked up to him, and they shook hands.

A moment later, Mac climbed up into the cab again. "He wants me to unload right here. I'll use my loader. If you'd like a drink or something, you're welcome in the office." He smiled at her. "I'll be in shortly. If you'd prefer, sit tight. I'm afraid it's either or."

"I'll stay in the cab then." She returned his smile.

"Fine. I won't be far." They shared another smile and Mac executed one of his graceful, no-motion-wasted exits. He loosened all his binders, then swung up to the seat of the loader. He set the outriggers. Then one log at a time, he unloaded his truck, adding to the pile on the ground. One by one, men wandered from the nearby buildings and watched the proceedings from a respectful distance. Bunks empty, he hoisted his trailer onto the front bunk and whisked himself to the ground.

A man wearing a light green, open-necked, sports shirt greeted Mac, as he reached the ground. "Thanks Mac. That's the best cedar we've seen in a long time."

"Thanks. There are two more loads coming next week just like this one. Coffee hot in the break room?"

"Sure, come on. Leave your truck there. We don't have another load coming in until yours next week."

Mac popped Elsie's door open and smiled up at her. "Come on, break time." He reached up for her and she slid into his arms. "Coffee and pop in the break room." Hand in hand they walked toward the nearby sheet metal building.

AFTER THE BREAK, THEY PULLED OUT OF THE SMALL MILL YARD, Mac asked, "Well, Elsie, would you like to go back to Newport the way we came or some other way?"

"Oh," she drew out the word. "How about a different way? I feel like seeing some more new country."

"Fine with me. I may haul a load over the Alsea, let's go back that way." Mac pointed the truck north on Highway 99 to Junction City. Just north of town, he swung onto Highway 99W toward Monroe.

He stopped there at a little place called Gramma's Kitchen that had two patrol cars, two log trucks and a tractor/semi-trailer rig parked outside. "Come on, I know it doesn't look like much, but they know how to feed a hungry man."

Inside he had to pay off two coffees to the police officers from the morning and everyone laughed over the whole episode. Mac and Elsie were just finishing their pie *a la mode*, or at least Mac was finishing off their pie *a la mode*, when a burly man in a shirt and tie and the two police officers stepped over to their table, laying a hand on the back of a chair. "May we sit down?" the burly man asked.

Mac shrugged. "Sure, what's up?" he asked.

"Well," began one of the officers, "We'd like to know more about your incident with this Mr. Pentice."

"You heard most of it. He started following me a little north of Seal Rock. I pulled off to show Elsie the rocks and waves there and he pulled in just as I was pulling out. I'm convinced he meant no harm, just couldn't figure out how to get to talk to me." Mac shrugged. "I certainly didn't drive like a normal log truck driver this morning, pulling off the highway to show off our coast like I did. I think he figured something was up when our parade arrived at the mill. He tried to pull out of line, but a pickup loaded with antennas boxed him back in." Mac chuckled.

The burly man reached across the table. "David Sharp," he began, "Pleased to meet you."

Mac raised his eyebrows and reached back. "Most people just call me Mac."

"Good to meet you. I've heard of you from other drivers and seen your truck up and down 101, but I've never had the pleasure of meeting you. I'm an enforcement officer with the U.S. Forest Service. The officers and I are checking trucks today for proper load identification, and in the case of Forest Service logs, haul routes and scaling points. In the past, there have been a few cases when high-priced timber has bypassed scaling stations. We don't suspect anyone at this time. However, our job is compliance. Should someone decide to direct loads to an unauthorized destination, Sam Pentice, as a freelance log buyer, would be a person of interest."

"No problem. I understand. Some of your new enforcement officers stop me, not believing I'm hauling my own timber. But all my timber I do cut off my own place."

"I know, but you haul out of the coast range and there's lots of cedar over there."

"True."

"We'd appreciate knowing if you see anything suspicious."

"Will do. We've got to get on the road. Good to meet you. I'm out Beaver Creek if you get over to that side of the mountains. Siuslaw National Forest, Waldport District." The men shared a smile.

"I'll be over in a couple weeks."

"Ah," the taller of the two policemen commented, "There's been a number of reports of bigfoot in the coast range, especially south of Newport."

"Oh?" Mac responded in supposed innocence.

"A few loggers have seen, or rather, glimpsed something that can only be explained as bigfoot or somebody in an ape suit."

"Are they dangerous?" Mac asked, doing his best to feign innocence.

The patrolmen shook their heads. "No one's been bothered by them. They seem to want to stay out of the way."

The other officer spoke up. "There's also been reports of fires in the night every so often in the woods in the coast range. Seems someone lights a great big bonfire around dusk and then puts it out by dawn. By the time we get there, there's just some trampled grass, but virtually no trace of a fire."

Mac raised his eyebrows. "And you think the fire is associated with the sasquatch?"

The officers shrugged. "We don't know," they admitted.

Mac smiled. "Thanks for the info. I'll keep a look out." Mac and Elsie shook hands all around and headed out.

As they cleared Monroe, Elsie broke the silence. "I believe you, Mac." She leaned against her door and watched him. He glanced across the cab and smiled.

"Thanks. I wasn't just seeing things. Oh, you've been near one too."

She startled and gasped. "I have?"

Mac chuckled. "Yes, remember that smell when we were walking back to the truck the day you were in the woods with me?"

Elsie nodded silently.

"That scent is a sasquatch."

"Oh." Her response was somewhere near an astonished whisper. "You're not afraid of them?"

Mac shook his head. "No. I'm nearly as big as the one that helped me free the little one caught in the rockslide. He is stronger than I am. At least, he could move larger rocks more easily than I could. Like the officer said, they seem to stay by themselves. People see them almost by accident."

Mac swung off 99W and onto the cut off to the Alsea highway. "I'm tempted to load again before I take you back to the motel," he muttered.

"I don't mind. I like the quiet of the woods."

"Okay. You haven't ridden in my other truck yet."

She looked at him in surprise and they shared a smile. Smiles that said parting would be difficult this evening.

CHAPTER 7

S unday evening, Mac settled back in his favorite chair. That afternoon, the weather had turned damp and cool. Out of habit, he lit a fire. He mused on the past week as he watched his fire and swished his coffee around in his cup. Elsie, ah Elsie! He couldn't help but smile at the thought of her. What was it about her? He'd taken out many a woman, but she was one of the very few who'd ever actually gotten into his house or especially his log truck.

And then there was the sasquatch. Somehow it had known he was trying to free the smaller one from the rockslide. He shivered in remembrance. There was something thrilling in having worked side-by-side with a wild creature. No, he wasn't afraid of the sasquatch. He trusted his fellow man less.

His mind flowed back to Elsie. How could he see her again? Monday he was taking the remaining two loads of cedar into Eugene. He wasn't figuring on taking anything into Willamina for a couple of weeks. His brow furrowed. Labor Day? Perhaps. He glugged his last two swallows of coffee, stood and hurried to the kitchen. Mac set his cup in the sink and studied his calendar.

Yeah, that would work. He'd call her Wednesday or Thursday evening.

THE FRIDAY BEFORE LABOR DAY WEEKEND, MAC STOPPED HIS empty log truck on the shoulder in front of Elsie's house. When traffic cleared, he whipped it around and backed into the drive. He set the brake, shut down the engine and gracefully swung out of the cab. Elsie met him as he rounded the rear of the truck. The smiles they shared were genuine, and the first touch of their hands sparked of an emotional electricity. "Hi, Elsie. Ready to go?" Mac asked, blushing.

She nodded. "Yes. Thank you for being willing to stay for dinner." She reached out her hand and Mac enclosed it in his own huge paw. "I found a job," she said with a thrill in her voice.

"Oh?"

"I'm the school nurse at the Willamina grade school."

"Great." Hand in hand they hurried to the front steps where Elsie's parents waited.

Mac shook hands with Fran and George. He snapped his fingers. "Opps. I brought some things out of my garden for you. Hang on." Mac jogged to the truck and lifted out a grocery sack. When he returned, he laid it in Fran's outstretched hands.

"What is this?" Fran asked.

"Some of the bounty from my land."

Fran peeked in. "Oh goody, cabbage and lettuce and … what's this package?" She lifted out a white, freezer-wrapped package.

"A venison roast for you to enjoy."

"Oh, thank you. I love things fresh from the garden!" She looked up and met Mac's eyes. "Please, come in."

"Thank you," Mac replied.

The four of them stepped into the living room, and as if by some prearranged signal, Elsie and her mother disappeared from the room. George motioned Mac to a have a seat. Mac glanced at him, then settled into the chair. Mac sighed as he wiggled a little, finding a comfortable position. "Even after sitting most of the day in a log truck, a comfy chair is still nice."

"Mac," George stated in all seriousness. "I can't stop Elsie from going with you for the weekend. But I'm concerned."

Mac smiled at his host. "George, no need. I would do nothing to ruin the relationship Elsie and I have, and I would do nothing to destroy the trust building between us."

George returned his smile. "Thanks. I trust you. I've met a few loggers in the last few weeks. They speak highly of you."

"Thank you. I'll do my best not to violate your trust either."

George stood. "Com'on, I think dinner is ready."

———————

As Mac pointed the truck toward the ocean on Highway 18, he glanced at Elsie. "I'm looking forward to this weekend."

"So am I." She smiled at him.

"Good. Your father is certainly protective of you. Though he admitted he couldn't really stop anything once we were outside his house."

Elsie sighed. "Yes, he is. In some ways I don't mind. I mean I don't want a relationship that is just physical. His attitude and sessions with the men who come for me weed out the less desirable ones in a hurry."

Mac chuckled. "Yes. Few men would stand for lectures on how to treat his daughter."

Elsie looked at him in shock. "Has he done that to you?"

"No lectures per se. He just says that I'm to be a gentleman around you and not to …" His voice faded out.

A thoughtful silence filled the cab. "And you said?"

"I'll do my best to uphold that standard. It's mine also."

"Thank you."

Silence again as Mac attended to the curves in the road. "What would you like to do this weekend?" he asked.

"Oh, I don't know. Walk the beach, hike in the woods, sample your cooking." They shared another smile. "Is there anything you have to do this weekend?"

"I have to haul back to Willamina Tuesday. So, I'd like to load Saturday morning. There's church on Sunday. I've been told the crabbing's good in Alsea Bay. Maybe, we can get some crab."

"That sounds like fun."

Little did they realize they'd get to load the truck, walk in the woods and go to church and that's about all. That other female would cross their tracks again.

CHAPTER 8

Saturday morning, Mac had the waffle iron hot and the griddle ready for homemade venison sausages, when Elsie appeared at the breakfast counter. Mac glanced up at her and smiled, approving her floor-length, blue, velour robe.

"Good morning, Elsie," Mac greeted her as she settled on one of the stools at the kitchen pass through and yawned. "Coffee?"

"Good morning, Mac. The coffee does smell good. Yes, please."

Mac poured a cup full and handed it to her. "The rest of breakfast will be along in a few minutes." He turned to the griddle and waffle iron.

Just before 9 a.m. that morning, they headed up one of his logging roads. He pulled past a landing full of logs, proceeded to a wider area, turned around and stopped next to the stack of logs. Just as he opened his door to swing up to the loader, Elsie gasped. "Mac, look!" She pointed down the road.

Mac turned. Running toward them, arms waving, came a large hairy human-ape figure. Mac recognized it as the large sasquatch he'd helped earlier in the month. "He's the one who helped with the rockslide, Elsie. He's running like a man in trouble or one who needs help. I'll see if I can figure out what he wants."

"Mac!" Elsie whispered.

"I'll be okay." He flashed her a reassuring smile. She returned a tiny one of her own.

Mac dropped to the ground and walked toward the creature. It stopped about 15 feet from him, grunting something that sounded like a language. Mac couldn't make heads or tails of it.

The creature raised his arm, like he was indicating something just a little smaller than himself. Then he clutched his calf. Mac nodded, realizing the creature was probably referring to the smaller sasquatch they'd saved out of the rockslide. Then it raised its arms like it held a rifle and made a noise like a shot. Mac tipped his head indicating he was still listening and trying to understand. After the sound of a shot, the creature grabbed his leg and sounded in pain. A moment later, it straightened as much as it could and looked at Mac with such a pleading in its eyes, Mac couldn't help but think of a father asking for help for his daughter.

Mac nodded. The creature smiled. Mac held up his hand trying to indicate a pause. He pointed to Elsie, then to himself and made the motions of walking. The sasquatch nodded in apparent understanding. Mac pivoted and jogged a few steps to Elsie's side of the cab. She sat still and pale, staring at their visitor. Mac jerked open her door and climbed halfway to the cab.

"Elsie!" Mac commanded with a quiet, no-nonsense voice. She jumped and whirled, looking down at him. "Grab the first aid kit. It's under the seat."

She unbuckled and reached down. After a moment of fumbling, she came up with a foot square, four-inch-thick, dusty, white, plastic box with a red cross on top. She handed it to him.

"Thanks. Now you see that red knob under the dash?" She looked and nodded.

"Pull it out. That's the engine shut off."

Elsie scooted over, grabbed the knob, grunted and pulled. The engine throbbed once more and was still.

"Good, now come." Her eyebrows rose.

"Me too?"

"Yes, you, too. You're the nurse. Come on."

Mac hopped to the ground, first aid kit under his arm. He reached up for Elsie. Quick and cautious, she clambered out. Mac shut the door with a thud. They hurried hand in hand to the waiting sasquatch. A look of relief flooded the creature's face. It turned and strode off down the road. Mac and Elsie followed, hurrying to the point of jogging. A dozen yards on, the creature looked back and motioned up the slope. Up it scrambled. Mac scrambled after it. Halfway up, he passed on the first aid kit to their guide then reached back for Elsie. The three of them moved off single file through the forest.

Ten minutes later they heard a low groaning. The sasquatch leading them grunted loudly, and they heard a scurrying of large creatures ahead of them.

The trio burst into a clearing. Off to one side, under the shelter of a crude lean-to made of cedar boughs, lay the smaller sasquatch that Mac had helped earlier, lying on a bed of ferns and evergreen boughs. The creature tossed and turned, twisted, and groaned. When it bumped a massive swelling on its leg, it let loose with a cry of pain that chilled Mac to the bone. Mac and Elsie shared a glance.

"Let's see what we can do," Mac commented. He stepped over to the creature and looked back at Elsie. She hadn't moved. "Elsie," Mac commanded. "Come here. This is bad, but I think we can lick it."

Elsie blinked and shook her head, then met Mac's eyes. She smiled a weak, uncertain smile and moved beside him, kneeling at the creature's foot. "It's badly infected. That's all. The bullet looks like it went through the muscle." With a soft and sensitive touch, Elsie ran her hand across the top of the leg. "I don't think it hit the bone. That's fortunate." The sasquatch gave a sudden, violent jerk, tearing its leg out of Elsie's grasp. "We've got to hold her still."

"Her?" Mac whispered in surprise.

"Yes, her. A woman can pick out another woman," Elsie responded as if Mac was just a bit thick-headed. "Now, to work." She flipped open the first aid kit and eyed its contents. "Mac, how sharp is your pocketknife?"

"Pretty sharp."

"Sharp enough to shave with?"

"There's a razor in the kit."

Elsie dug through it a little and came up with a razor blade. "I'd rather use your knife."

Mac fished it out of his pocket and handed it to Elsie. She opened it and tested the edge on her thumbnail. "It'll do. Now hold her still."

Mac motioned the other sasquatch over to them. Mac grabbed the injured leg and motioned it must stay still. The creature nodded and held the small one down at the hips.

With slow and gentle strokes, she began to shave the area around the wound. The patient screamed once and tried to escape. Finally, she had a bare area around the bullet hole. Fire red lines barely visible against dark skin spider-webbed away from the wound. She turned to Mac, "Have you got a match or lighter on you?"

"There are matches in the first aid kit."

Again, Elsie dug through and found the matches in an old, Boy Scout, waterproof container. She took one out, struck it and held it under the knife blade. A moment later, she lanced the wound with a deft touch like she'd done it a million times. A stream of yellow liquid surged out, then began to drip. The creature screamed, then lay still as the pressure on her leg eased. "Hold her still," Elsie commanded in a no-nonsense tone. Moving to the creature's head, she touched her forehead. Elsie held her hand there a moment. Then, she lay her fingertips on the forehead of the sasquatch, who was helping them. "Mac, she's got a dangerously high fever. We've got to cool her off."

Mac nodded acknowledgment in silence. Then he had an idea. He pulled out his large handkerchief and laid it on the hands of the larger sasquatch. When it met his eyes, Mac wiped his brow like he was hot, reached for the handkerchief, wrung it out, placed it on his forehead and sighed in pretend relief, then handed the handkerchief back to the creature. It gave him a blank look. Mac again pantomimed wringing the cloth out, this time placing it on their patient's forehead. The larger creature nodded, took the handkerchief and disappeared into the woods.

"Mac, what are we going to do? We need so much more, but we don't have it."

"What do we need?"

"Hot compresses for the leg, cold compresses to try to lower her fever, aspirin, antibiotics would help." Her voice held a desperate plea.

Mac met her eyes. The plea shone out from them too. He looked away. "I could go get my camp stove and some water and pots to warm it in. And I've got a few penicillin pills at the house."

Elsie sighed. "Go get them. Go quickly!" A rustling in the brush turned their attention from their patient.

The larger sasquatch stepped into the clearing. It handed the dripping handkerchief to Elsie. Elsie smiled up in gratitude and laid the cloth on her patient's forehead. She sighed in relief. The larger sasquatch smiled too.

Mac got its attention, pointed to himself, made walking motions with his fingers away from them and then back. He pointed to Elsie and held up his hand in a "stay" signal. The sasquatch nodded.

Mac squatted next to Elsie. "I'll be back as quick as I can. Hopefully, in the next 15 minutes but maybe as long as an hour or more. I will be back."

"Thank you. Please hurry. Bring whatever you think will help."

Mac nodded. They shared a quick kiss, and Mac left the clearing. A few minutes later, Elsie thought she heard Mac's truck pass by.

At the house, Mac gathered everything he thought they'd need and then some, loaded it all in his pickup and headed back into the woods. When he returned to the clearing, he set up his camp stove and put on a small pot of water. They managed to get their patient to swallow two aspirin and one penicillin pill. With the cold compresses on her forehead, her temperature retreated. The hot compresses and hydrogen peroxide eased the infection in her leg. With the help of the larger sasquatch, they got her to drink. Though drinking from a cup seemed to be a new experience.

Around 2 o'clock that afternoon, Elsie told Mac, "I think she's out of danger, Mac. Her fever's down. I just hope it stays there. The infection is beginning to retreat from her leg."

"Can we leave her?"

Elsie shook her head. "If it were my child, I wouldn't. So, no. I can't."

"Okay. I've brought a little bit to eat, if you're hungry. I can change compresses for a while. You're bushed."

She smiled a smile that melted Mac's heart. "Thank you."

Mac flipped out a heavy blanket he'd brought. "Here, you can watch your patient and everything."

Like he thought, she fell asleep within minutes, after she'd eaten and lay down. He knew this had been an exhausting morning for her.

The other sasquatch tended the cold compresses, as Mac fished out another hot one from the water on the stove and laid it on the patient's wound. He thought over what he had brought with him to eat tonight. Yes, they'd have enough for another day, but not much more.

The big sasquatch grunted, and Mac looked up into its eyes. Something akin to tears glistened on their surface. Mac nodded and smiled. Somehow Mac knew they were tears of relief, and these two creatures were related. They reacted to each other too much like family.

The big sasquatch grunted again and drew Mac's attention. It pointed to itself and grunted "Oogla." Mac stared blankly a moment, as the creature repeated itself. Then it pointed to the patient and grunted "Oona." Mac startled, as it pointed to him. Slowly Mac understood.

He pointed to himself and said "Mac." Oogla got out "Mauk." Mac smiled and nodded his head. Mac pointed to Elsie. "Elsie," he said.

"Else," struggled off Oogla's tongue.

Mac smiled again and began to chuckle. Oogla began to join in. This definitely wasn't going to be a dull few days stuck in the woods. They were going to learn a new language and culture.

CHAPTER 9

By the time Elsie woke up from her nap, Mac had figured out Oogla's language to be a combination of signs and sounds. Oogla had given him a thorough introduction, and Mac pretty well conquered the simplistic fundamentals. Surprisingly, Oogla managed a few simple words in English. Elsie woke with a start, as Oogla stepped back into the clearing with a pail full of blackberries. Mac grunted a heartfelt thank you in sasquatch. Oogla smiled. Elsie stared at Mac a moment.

"They do have a language then?" she asked in a whisper. "He looked like he understood what you said. I certainly didn't."

Mac grinned at her. "Our patient is improving little by little. And yes, Oogla has a language."

"Oogla?" she responded in an astonished whisper.

"Yes, this is Oogla," Mac answered, motioning. "And our patient is Oona." Elsie looked at him wide-eyed and open-mouthed. Finally, her jaw clicked shut.

"How many more of them are there?"

Mac shrugged. "I don't know. I haven't figured out how to ask." He smiled at Elsie, and they shared a kiss.

After checking her patient, Elsie noticed the pan in his hands. "What are you doing?" she asked.

"Making dinner," he responded as if primitive camping and cooking was an everyday affair. "Though right now I'm making dessert. Oogla just brought us some blackberries. I'm starting on blackberry dumplings."

"What's for dinner?"

"Steak. I have some chicken soup heating for Oona."

She smiled at him, "Thank you."

So went the rest of Saturday. Elsie agreed to first watch, Oogla middle and Mac the early morning watch. As darkness began to gather about them, Elsie looked around her. "Are we staying here?"

"Yes," Mac answered with a chuckle. "There's plenty of blankets and a sleeping bag. Take your pick."

Elsie stammered a moment. "I ... I wasn't concerned about bedding. It's being out here like this in the woods."

"Rest assured nothing will happen to us, not with Oogla and clan guarding us. We have quite a stack of firewood. Now, how do you want the bed?" Mac held the sleeping bag roll in his hands.

Elsie gave him a sideways glance. "Depends on whether or not you intend to keep your agreement with Father and me."

A smile crept across his face as he met her eyes. "I intend to keep it."

"Then let me help." She spread the plastic sheet under the canvas lean-to Mac had set up. She flipped a couple blankets over the plastic, then they unrolled the sleeping bag together, unzipped it and spread it wide over the blankets. Elsie rolled another small blanket into a pillow. She tipped back on her heels. "There, I understand I'm on first watch." Mac nodded and added a couple sticks to the fire. He settled on the end of the sleeping bag next to Elsie. "Not exactly the weekend I'd planned, should I apologize?"

They both stared into the small fire, flickering before them. "No," Elsie responded, drawing out the word in thought. "Don't apologize. It's been worth it."

Their eyes met and then their lips. Elsie pulled away when Oona stirred and groaned. "Excuse me, I need to tend our patient."

Mac watched in silence as she checked Oona's leg and temperature. He had the feeling the halting conversation between the two women would go on forever. As he began to unlace his boots, he felt Oogla settle beside him.

"Many thanks," Oogla grunted. Mac turned to meet the tear-filled eyes.

"Many pleasures," Mac returned.

They watched as Elsie slipped half a blanket under Oona, then folded the rest over her. Oona sighed. So did Oogla. "You save Oona. Lose too many."

"You learn to heal," Elsie responded from across the little clearing. "You try your cures. We finish your work." Elsie settled next to Oogla. "You know many medicines in woods. You teach me, I teach you."

Silence, except for the whisper of the breeze in the treetops, the crackle of the small fire and the call of an owl. "You, hairless one. I, man of forest. Hard to ask."

Elsie squeezed his knee. "Thank you for asking. You, Oona friends."

"Yes. Friends. I afraid. Oona knows only you friends. I know you friends. New ones think all hairless ones friends."

Mac sighed. "Yes, Oogla. Elsie and I rare hairless ones. Best keep separate." Mac met Oogla's eyes. "Your family, my family friends."

"Friends," Oogla added with a decisive nod.

Mac finished unlacing his boots, crawled to Elsie behind Oogla and kissed her cheek. "Good night." He yawned, shed his jacket and crawled under the sleeping bag. He listened a few minutes to Elsie and Oogla's quiet halting conversation until sleep claimed him. Sometime later, he felt Elsie slip in beside him. He rolled over and enclosed her in his arms. They both slept.

By noon Sunday, Oona's temperature seemed normal and her leg was well on its way to being healed. Communicating with Mac and Elsie seemed her primary interest. Elsie in particular. Elsie checked her out one last time as Mac packed up their temporary camp. They agreed to meet on the road at high noon Monday.

At the truck, Oogla communicated with Mac, "Else, mate?"

Mac stared at him a moment then smiled. "No, not yet. A few moons perhaps. Thank you for help."

"Thank you. You save Oona."

Mac and Elsie made it to an evening church service.

ON MONDAY AT NOON, THEY MET OOGLA AND OONA AT THE appointed time and place. Oogla took Mac aside and asked, "Mauk and Else come to celebration?"

"Celebration? Place and when?"

"Day and night same length."

"We come. Where?"

"Meet you where road crosses ridge."

"Old road. No one use?"

"Yes."

"We be there."

"Many men of woods there."

———————————

THAT EVENING OVER DINNER, MAC COMMENTED, "WELL, ELSIE, do you believe me now that sasquatch are real?"

She smiled at him. "Yes. I'm glad we were able to help. Will we see them again?"

Mac grinned back. "Oh yes. We've been invited to the fall equinox celebration. I guess, it's the night of September 21. I'll pick you up at school that night." He checked his calendar. "It's a Friday."

"What's going to happen?"

Mac shrugged. "I don't know. Oogla asked that we be at the high road at sunset. That reminds me, we need to be on the road by 6 a.m. tomorrow to get you to work by 8 a.m. So, breakfast at 5:30 a.m."

She yawned. "I'll try to be ready."

Early in the evening they shared a kiss and slipped into their separate rooms. Sometime a little after midnight, Mac heard light footsteps in the living room. Half asleep, he remembered Elsie was in the house. She must be headed to or from the bathroom. A moment later a shriek jolted him the rest of the way awake. Elsie dashed through his doorway and flew under his covers, hugging his back, arms around his chest. She quivered like something dreadful had happened. He disentangled her arms and rolled over to face her.

"Elsie," he whispered, "What's the matter?"

"There's a b-b-bear in your living room," she stuttered, hugging him close.

Mac smiled and chuckled softly. "You're right. There's a bear in my living room."

She pushed away from him a little. "There is?"

"Yes. My bear rug."

Mac felt the warmth of her blush. He laid a soft kiss on her forehead, rolled onto his back, and drew her to him. Her head rested on his broad shoulder. Her slim body stretched out quivering beside him. As they talked, her quivering slowed until she lay still and warm. "Elsie, you're not the first to stick your foot in that bear's mouth."

"I'm not?" she responded in a whisper.

"No. I think most of my nieces and nephews have done it, plus my sister-in-law" They lay in silence many moments. "Elsie." Mac whispered.

"Hum?" she responded half asleep.

"Your father told me distinctly that I was not to take you to my bed before our wedding night." Mac felt her stiffen a little. "Two things. One, you came to me. And two, I will not make you stay." He loosened his hold on her. She cuddled closer.

They shared another kiss. She rolled over, and he enclosed her in his arms. Mac slept better that night than he had for at least two weeks.

———————————

THEY PULLED OUT A FEW MINUTES LATE TUESDAY MORNING, and Mac let Elsie off in front of her school before he stopped by the log dump.

They shared a kiss in the cab of his truck in front of Willamina grade school. The milling students seemed to cease all activity as Elsie swung down to the ground. She waved as Mac pulled out. He'd drop her suitcase off at her house after he unloaded.

CHAPTER 10

The afternoon of the 21st, Mac pulled up in front of the school. He set the brakes and poured himself a cup of coffee out of his thermos. He waved to the last school bus out. A teacherly looking person wandered toward him. He swung out of the truck and met her by the passenger door.

"May I help you?" she asked, with a tone of voice that said log trucks, even empty ones, weren't really welcome outside her school.

Mac smiled. "I'm waiting for your nurse, Elsie Turnupseed."

The lady smiled at last. "Ah, you must be Mac. Come on in. I'll show you where her office is."

Mac locked up the cab and followed the lady into the school, where he met Elsie. To his surprise, he also met several wives of truckers and mill workers he knew. They shared a laugh. Then he and Elsie hurried out the door, hand in hand.

"Well," he began when they'd hit the road to the beach, "how were your first few weeks of school?"

"Pretty good. Nothing as serious as Oona's flesh wound. Mostly, the typical scraped and sprained elbows and knees." They both laughed. "I decided to let everyone call me Miss Elsie. It's a lot easier for the little ones than Miss Turnupseed."

After dinner, they took the pickup to the top of the ridge and watched the sunset over the ocean. Just before dark, Oogla appeared out of nowhere and called to them. They followed him in silence as he walked down the overgrown evergreen lined road. Oogla led them through the forest on a nearly invisible trail. Suddenly they came out into a large clearing. Mac knew this place well. Often, he'd hunted here. It was a bowl, ridges on all sides with only one small stream forcing its way through a narrow ravine on the north side.

A huge bonfire in the center of the clearing caught their attention. The flames illuminated at least two dozen sasquatch circling the fire. Each held the next by the hand. They circled left and kicked, then circled right and kicked. The dance fascinated Mac. There was a primitive gracefulness in their movements. Then they caught the feel of drums. Big drums! They were felt more than heard. Elsie tightened her grip on Mac's hand.

They glanced at each other. "Fires in the night!" whispered Elsie.

Smiling in awareness, Mac nodded his agreement.

Oogla stopped and looked back at them. "Fear?"

Mac shook his head. "New. Do not know dance."

Oogla shook his head. "Watch. Dance. Food and drink." He pointed to a smaller fire off to one side.

Oona sorted herself out of the crowd, dragging another sasquatch toward them. "Mauk and Else!" she exclaimed growling and grunting in her sasquatch way. "My mate in several moons." She indicated the male beside her. "Shule."

Shule stood over a foot taller than Mac, dark brown, almost black hair. A splendid example of his species. Mac reached out a sasquatch greeting Oogla had shown him.

Shule scowled. "You, hairless ones. You go."

"I save Oona twice. Once with Else's help. Oogla invite."

Without warning, Shule leapt at Mac. Mac dodged and tripped up the young sasquatch. In an instant, they were grappling on the ground. With the first tussle, Mac realized Shule had the reach and strength on him, but he was quicker. One feint and Mac pinned Shule to the ground. "Mac and Elsie celebrate now?" Mac growled.

Shule grunted his reluctant assent.

"Oona yours. Elsie mine. Peace?"

"Peace," Shule grunted.

Mac let him up and greeted him again. Shule smiled and greeted him as an equal. The foursome joined the circling group.

As he and Elsie danced around the fire, the others greeted them and laughed at their clumsy first efforts. Mac relaxed when he realized the laughter was all in good fun and included plenty of good-natured encouragement.

Laughing and tired, Mac and Elsie settled outside the ring. Someone brought them a wooden bowl full of a warm drink smelling of honey. Sharing the bowl, they both took a sip, then after a glance, drank the bowl empty. As they watched, Elsie commented, "That was quite a greeting Shule gave you. Do you think it was a setup?"

Mac nodded and grinned. "He could have torn me apart, if he'd really wanted to. It was a test."

"It's obvious you passed."

"And having Oogla invite us helped too."

"Oh?"

"More than one has asked how we got here. They welcome me, when I tell them Oogla invite." A new circle formed before them. "Come on!" Elsie exclaimed, "This is fun!" She pulled him up, they left their coats on the ground and joined in. Again, the jovial, kindly assistance. Mac glanced at Elsie. She smiled at him. Her smile showed she was enjoying herself as much as he was. Her face gleamed of perspiration in the glow of the firelight. A few beads ran down her neck into her shirt. Her blonde hair flowed out behind her, then twisted around her neck as the circle changed directions. There was something desirable and very sensuous about her tonight.

Another rest and drink of the honey-scented liquid. "What is it?" she asked as she leaned on him.

"I think it's a primitive mead."

"Mead?! The stuff the Vikings drank?"

"The very same."

Another drink and they stumbled through another dance. Mac led her off to a slight rise, where they could sit and watch. Far enough away not to be stepped on, yet near enough to catch a little of the heat from the fire.

"Whash a night!" Elsie slurred. "I won't ever forget … it." She leaned her head on Mac's shoulder, then collapsed in his lap.

Alarmed, Mac checked her pulse and breathing. Just fine. Then the mead hit him too. Somehow, he arranged her in his arms and laid beside her. The beat of the drums and wild calls from around the fire faded from his consciousness.

Mac shivered, slowly opened his eyes and looked around him. His head hurt. A graceful deer stepping across his front lawn would have sounded like a herd of charging elk. This was the kind of morning when cats tromping across carpeting woke you up. The clearing. Yes, that's where they still were. Elsie stirred in his arms, her hair cascading over his arm. The sun poked its top edge over the trees. Somewhere around 7 a.m., Mac figured. But what day? It hurt to move. As gently as he could, he laid his head back down. He was grateful someone had thrown their coats over them.

Elsie stirred again. "Mac," she said as if her head hurt as bad as his. "Where are we?"

"In the clearing."

"Did we really dance the night away? With sasquatch?"

"Yes, we did."

She rolled over in his arms to face him. "How are we going to explain?"

"Explain what?"

"How we spent the night."

"I don't see we have to. I don't think we slept the whole weekend away."

At last, she opened her eyes. Then snapped them shut. "Ow! The sun is bright!"

Mac propped himself up on one elbow to shield her face from the rising sun. "Now, try again," he whispered. He smiled as her blue eyes shone up at him. They closed again as he bent down and kissed her.

She smiled as he drew away. "I hate to think what Father would say, if he knew what we've been up to tonight. That mead must have been powerful stuff."

Mac smiled, and they shared another kiss. Then he sat up and scanned the clearing, his hunting mind on alert. A deer across the clearing, jerked its head up, its big ears pivoted toward them like radar antennas. Mac stood and the deer bolted for the woods. He reached down, and she allowed him to help her up. She wobbled a moment, and then they reached an arm around each other's waist.

They stopped by the fire pit. Very little trace remained of their monstrous bonfire. "I wonder how they do it?" Mac mused.

Elsie looked up at him, and her movement drew his attention. She smiled. "Maybe it wasn't real," she whispered.

"No, I'm very sure it's real. That mead sunk in too well."

They both smiled, and then shared a kiss. "Come, let's see if we can make it back to the pickup."

"I'm glad you know where it is."

"I'm pretty sure at least." They chuckled again and together, watching every step, moved out of the clearing.

CHAPTER 11

Through October and November, Mac met Elsie for lunch at the school as often as he could. His green log truck became a familiar sight.

They spent Thanksgiving in Sheridan with her parents. Then Friday, Elsie and Mac made the short journey to Kelso, Washington, to spend a day with Mac's sister, Jill, her husband, Jack, and their children—Jenny 10, Josh 8, and Janice 4.

As they rode back to Sheridan, Elsie asked, "Mac, you haven't invited me to your place for quite a while." There was a quiet hurt in her voice. A pensive questioning deeper than her words.

"No, Elsie, I haven't. Do you know I care for you?"

"Oh, yes!"

"That's why."

"I don't understand!"

"Elsie, I care very much about you. After spending now three or four nights with you in my arms, that's where I want you. But I also know how difficult it was not to go too far a couple of those nights."

"I wonder," she sighed.

"I don't, Elsie. I know," Mac responded with a conviction that caused Elsie to turn and look at him.

"Why do you know?" Elsie wondered out loud. She paused, then continued. "You don't have to answer, if you don't want to."

"No, our relationship is to a point it should come out." Mac paused and took a deep breath. "When I was about 20, I loved a girl very much. We made love one night, and it destroyed our relationship. She was a special lady—until that night. Something happened. I saw her once more. Then she moved away, and I lost track of her." He caressed the top of Elsie's head with his cheek. She leaned against him.

"Thank you, Mac." Her chuckle was so soft Mac almost didn't hear it. "It's strange. Most men are willing to take a woman to bed on the slightest notice, but here you're afraid of doing just that."

"Afraid of that before we're married," he chortled. Elsie jumped and looked at him in alarm. He smiled at her, and she relaxed beside him.

They rode in silence. Mac could almost feel Elsie fighting with herself about something but decided to let it come out on its own.

"Mac," she began, soft and serious. "I won't come to your bed a virgin." She swallowed hard, and Mac almost stepped on her words as she continued. "I loved a young man, and he coaxed me into bed with him. That's all he wanted from then on. When I insisted that we wait until we were married, he didn't want anything more to do with me." She sniffled. Mac rubbed his cheek on her hair again.

"Elsie," Mac responded with his gentlest tone, "Thank you for telling me. But it doesn't make any difference in my opinion of you. You're a very special lady to me."

"Thank you, Mac."

"Is that the reason you still live at home?"

"Yes. You're one of the few men I've trusted enough to develop a relationship with. Thank you."

SUNDAY AFTER SUPPER, ELSIE WALKED MAC BACK TO HIS PICKUP. "I'll keep in touch Elsie, but I won't be up very often before Christmas. I've a large contract to keep with Mapleton. While I've got most of it cut, I don't have a lot of it yarded. I'll call. Thanks for being willing to come Christmas. I think all of my family will be there. I'll be happy to come get you the afternoon school is out. That way we can have a few days to ourselves before everyone gets there." He looked into those unhappy blue eyes. "It's only three weeks," he pleaded.

"It will be three of the longest weeks of my life."

"Mine too, but it must be." He drew her into a close embrace. She hugged him back. After a couple minutes, he released her. They shared a long kiss, then he slid into the pickup. "I'll see you." They shared another longing smile, then another kiss and he pulled out of the drive. One more wave and she was out of sight.

As Mac worked in the woods, then hauled his timber to Mapleton, he thought a lot about Elsie. The mere fact she'd even consider aiding an injured sasquatch spoke highly of her. And then having enough nerve to dance with them. He smiled to himself in remembrance of that night.

Rainy, stormy evenings in front of his fireplace somehow seemed emptier than ever before.

Oogla helped out in the woods a couple of times. Mac brought down a deer for him in return. Strange, thought Mac, to have a friend that's supposedly a legendary creature. They talked many an hour up in the woods. Mac learned many forest skills and sharpened several others. His greatest satisfaction came one afternoon when he snuck up on Oogla undetected, using skills that Oogla taught him.

But it was Oona who seemed to actively seek Mac out. She'd ask about Elsie, and they'd talk a bit before she'd disappear back into the woods. Her enthusiasm for Shule often sent Mac musing on Elsie. Would Elsie make a good wife? Would she be willing to live out in the woods? To garden? To haul wood?

Then one day as he was loading his truck, the answer hit him like a thunderclap—YES!

The next questions he had to answer was, would he make a good husband for Elsie? And did he love her? Those were harder to answer. He knew he was willing to try to be a good husband. But love? He had thought he loved Joyce, but this thing with Elsie felt different from then. Love? The Bible says love is patient, kind, it does not envy. Love does not delight in evil but rejoices in truth. It always protects, always trusts, always hopes, always perseveres. Yes, his feelings for Elsie fulfilled all those qualifications.

That decided, he made a stop in Florence and looked over rings. He felt rather self-conscious and conspicuous, as he hunkered his big frame over the display cases.

"May I help you?" a stylish lady clerk well over a foot shorter than Mac asked.

Mac swallowed and blushed, "Well, I'm looking for an engagement ring."

The lady smiled and nodded her head in acknowledgment. "That's apparent. Any preferences?"

"Oh, yes, I know which lady I prefer." Mac blushed a deeper shade of red and glanced up. He could tell the clerk was struggling not to laugh and was grateful she didn't. "She's tall and slender with very long slender hands." He held up one of his own huge paws. "Her fingers come to here, just short of my own fingertips."

Finally, he settled on a ring with a small oval dark blue star sapphire flanked by two small diamonds. Yes, that would do. The sapphire matched the blue of her eyes. As he wrote the check, the clerk wrapped the small velvet box holding the ring. He gently placed the package in his jacket pocket, buttoned it closed, thanked the clerk and strode out the door.

That evening at home, Mac checked his calendar. Wednesday. Let's see, pick up Elsie tomorrow at 3:30 p.m., four more loads to Mapleton before the new year. He'd make one run tomorrow morning. The others not til a couple days after Christmas, because his nieces and nephews always wanted a ride in his log truck.

His sister and brother with their families were due to arrive Sunday evening. Elsie's folks would be down Monday. Christmas was Tuesday. Yes, he'd make enough time before Christmas to pop the question before everyone descended on his place.

CHAPTER 12

On Thursday morning, Mac delivered his load to Mapleton, and then hurried home. Just after lunch, he climbed into his pickup and headed for Sheridan and Elsie's house. He knew George was on swing shift this week. Mac glanced at his watch as he pulled into Elsie's drive at 2 p.m. Just a touch more than an hour to pick up Elsie. At his knock, Fran opened the door.

"Mac!" she exclaimed in surprise. "I didn't expect to see you until Monday, when we come to your place." She stepped back. "Please, come in. Can I get you anything?"

Mac smiled as he stepped in. "No thanks, I'm due at Elsie's school around three-thirty. I need to talk to George."

Fran's straw-colored eyebrows rose. "Do I get to listen in?" she teased him as they walked side-by-side to the kitchen.

"As far as I'm concerned," Mac teased back.

George stood as they entered. "Welcome Mac. I'm looking forward to coming down for Christmas." The two men shook hands over the table.

"I'm looking forward to having you, but it's going to be quite a houseful. Don't be surprised if my nieces and nephews call you Gramma and Grampa. They don't remember their own very well, and every now and then pine for them."

"It would be my pleasure. What can I do for you?"

Mac swallowed hard. "Well, I was wondering if you'd be willing to allow me a forever Christmas present. I'd like to ask Elsie to marry me. And if I remember protocol, I'm supposed to ask the lady's father." It all came out in a rush, and Mac swallowed again.

George chuckled. "Yes, Mac. I give you permission to marry Elsie." Fran clapped her hands twice, let loose with a soft little, happy squeal and bounced on her toes. "I've met few men I'm more willing to have my daughter marry." They shook hands again. "Though, I really couldn't deny you, if you pushed it."

Mac grinned. "I know. But I thought you might like to know my intentions toward your daughter are honorable. Thank you for your confidence. I'll take good care of her. With everything that goes on around my place, she'll get to earn her keep. But I don't see anything wrong with that."

"Mac!" Fran protested in such a way, the men laughed. "You'd better take care of her!"

Mac turned to her, picked her up and gave her a crushing hug. "There are women who would love to live out at my place with the quiet and the quality of life. But there's work. In the summer, there's food to put up. In the fall, there's meat to freeze. All winter there's wood to haul for the fireplace. It's not an easy life, but it's a good life. Plus, the man of the house likes to come home at night." He smiled and winked, then set her back down. "Besides, where else can I get a mother-in-law like you?"

Fran tipped her head and gave him a suspicious look, a smile teasing the corners of her mouth. "And how am I supposed to take that?"

"In good humor." Mac said. George chuckled when Fran burst out laughing and jabbed at Mac's ribs. "Thank you. I will take good care of Elsie. She's very special to me." He turned to leave, then stopped. "Oh, do you have a chain saw, George?"

"No. Why?"

"Well, it's become tradition, I give my family about three cords of wood every Christmas. How it works is I take one day and make a run through the valley with my log truck loaded with alder. I drop a little off at my sister's place, then my brother's. They cut it up themselves after I drop it off. I'm willing to do the same for you if you're interested."

"Can I tell you when we see you next?"

"Sure. Bring your pickup and we'll load it before you head home."

"Great. This wood heat business is new to us."

"See you Monday. Dinner at six."

Another handshake with George and a hug from and for Fran, Mac stepped out onto the porch and strode to his pickup.

Just as he closed the pickup door, Fran burst out of the house with a large box in her arms. "Mac! Elsie wants this. It's Christmas decorations she thought would work at your house."

Mac grinned, and they slid the box in the back. "Thanks. See you Monday." Another wave and he was off for Elsie.

Three-twenty on the dot he pulled up and parked in the parking lot for a change. Elsie stood talking with another teacher, oblivious to the forest-green pickup. Mac slipped through a back door and came up unbeknownst behind the two women. He scooped Elsie up in his arms and kissed her before she could react. The teacher jumped in surprise.

"Mac!" Elsie protested from his arms. "How did you sneak in?"

"I didn't bring the log truck."

"Oh." They shared another, gentler kiss.

"Are you ready to go?"

"Yes."

"Good." Mac nodded to the teacher. "I'll have her back by the time school starts next year." He winked at her.

"Mac! Put me down!" Elsie protested again. "Look at all the kids."

Teasing, he asked, "What about them?" as he strode off toward his pickup, Elsie still in his arms.

"They're staring!"

"Oh, all right. As long I get one more kiss before I set you down." Elsie blushed as he suited action to words. He tipped her out of his arms, keeping hold of her hand. Mac opened the passenger door with a great flourish. Elsie blushed again as she buckled into the right-hand seat belt. "There's a middle one," he teased.

She eyed him, head tipped. "I'll consider it later on. But not here in public."

They shared a giant pizza at Abby's Pizza in Newport and drove through the thick Oregon mist to Mac's place. He parked the pickup and they jogged through the drizzle to the back porch. Mac opened the door and they shared a kiss as Elsie stepped past him into the dark house. As they rounded the corner out of the kitchen into the dining area, Elsie teased him, "Which room do I put my suitcase in?"

"I'd like to say mine, but really, the guest room. Though you'll probably get a corner of the loft after everyone gets here."

"Why?"

He set the box of decorations on the dining table and turned to her. "Your folks need a place to sleep as do both my brother and sister. The double beds are in the guest room and the Hide-A-Bed in the living room. My brother's bringing his travel trailer, so he's taken care of."

"Oh." She paused and looked around the room, stopping when she met his eyes. "Who else gets the loft?"

"My nieces and nephews. The unmarried kids."

She smiled. "And I'm an unmarried kid?"

Mac blushed. "Well, unmarried this Christmas at least."

"And what makes you think I'll be married next Christmas?" She pressed on with her tease, enjoying the awareness that she was putting him on the spot.

Mac took the suitcase out of her hands and set it down. He reached both hands to her, and she took them. "Elsie," he responded in a near whisper, looking into her eyes, "I was hoping to find a more romantic spot, but Elsie, would you marry me?" He swallowed. "That way we'll know in advance whether you'll be married next Christmas."

"I'm sorry, I didn't mean to push you. I was just teasing."

"That may be, but I'm not. Please, just answer my question." They shared a shy smile.

This time, Elsie swallowed. "Yes, Mac. I would be pleased and honored to be your wife," she responded in a whisper.

"Thank you." They stood a moment looking deep into each other's eyes, then Mac drew her into an embrace tight against him.

Elsie's shiver brought them back to reality. "I'm sorry, but the house is cold. Let me light a fire," Mac said as he gave her one last squeeze and stepped over to the fireplace insert, flipping on a light as he passed an end table.

CHAPTER 13

With Elsie's stuff in the guest bedroom, they watched the fire from the love seat. They talked of life, expectations, dreams, things appropriate for a newly engaged couple. Mac shared his schedule, winter storms and the work of living out there.

"Mac," Elsie sighed. "Like you say, it takes work to live out here, but I'm willing. What I don't know, I'm willing to learn. Mother and I have done some canning and freezing. I'm not totally new to all that." She looked up and smiled at him. "Can Mother come sometimes and help?"

"Help with what?" he replied, a twinkle in his eyes.

"The canning and putting food by."

"Of course. Your mother is willing to become my mother-in-law."

She jabbed for his ribs, but he jumped out of her way and caught her hands. "Come, it's time to hit the sack. I've got to load the truck tomorrow or Saturday. I'd just as soon do it tomorrow. Besides, I'd like to bring a load of alder down too." He bent and kissed her gently. "No feet in bear's mouths tonight, okay?"

She blushed and looked up with a shy smile. "Ah, shucks, I like how you reassured me."

"I did too. But tonight, the temptation to break our agreement is far too strong. I'm loathe to disappoint your father." He stood and pulled her up.

"Thank you, Mac." Another kiss and a hug. He turned her and gave her a gentle shove toward the guest room.

Friday mid-morning they wound their way into the woods and hauled out a load of alder. Elsie tried her hand at the loader when they unloaded the truck next to Mac's woodshed. He grinned at her, squeezed her shoulder and told her, "Good job. Thank you for being so willing to learn." They shared a smile and kiss.

Then back to the woods for his Wednesday load of fir. From his perch high on the loader, he pointed and called, "It's Oona!"

Elsie ran to greet her friend. In moments they were chattering in a combination of sign language, sasquatch and pidgin English. Mac had to smile. He waved to Oogla as the bigger, older sasquatch stepped onto the road behind the two women. Mac paused. Those two females. How they had affected his life.

He looked forward to life with Elsie. He had been content with life before she came along, but she filled a void he had only suspected lay hidden within him.

And Oona. If she hadn't been caught in that slide, he'd never met Oogla. That creature was wise in the ways of the woods. Getting his deer and elk had never before been easier. They shared the concern that Oona desired to learn too much of the ways of the "hairless ones." Each species had much to share with the other but where to draw the line?

Oogla strode past Elsie and Oona. He waited while Mac loaded the last log, then tucked the loader away in its traveling position. Together they snugged down the load. "Thank you," Mac said, giving the big sasquatch a gentle punch on the shoulder.

Oogla smiled. "Mauk, you new man. What happen?"

Mac laughed. "Elsie my mate in few moons."

Oogla grunted, then thought a minute. "You come, Oona's mating celebration?"

Mac met his eyes. "When?"

"Night after longest day."

"What happen?"

"Dance around fire. Send new couple to woods alone."

"No more?"

Oogla shook his head, a habit he'd picked up. "No more."

Mac grinned. "We come."

"You come to spring celebration?"

Mac shook his head. "No. Not safe for me and Elsie to be together like that until mated by hairless one's rules."

Oogla registered alarm. "Safe from man of woods."

Mac nodded and grinned. "Yes. Elsie not safe from me. I like Elsie very much."

Oogla nodded and smiled, as if he understood the young of the species. "Me go. Else good mate for Mauk."

They shared a smile. Oogla turned and started up the road. He made a motion to Oona and continued on. A minute later, Oona too turned and joined the older sasquatch. The two couples waved to each other, and then Oona and Oogla vanished into the woods. Elsie, deep in thought, wandered back to where Mac was waiting beside his idling truck. He reached out a hand to her and she reached back.

"Never thought you'd have a friend of a different species, did you?"

Elsie looked back toward where the two had vanished. She shook her head in amazement. When she turned to face Mac, she smiled. "No, I didn't. Maybe someday we can tell the tales."

"I hadn't thought of it like that. I'm sure our grandchildren will thrill to them."

"Yes. I'm looking forward to that." He drew her to him and cradled her head in a classic Hollywood embrace. When they came up for air, they stood a moment, Elsie resting her head on his shoulder.

"Come, we've one more errand today."

"Oh?" She tipped her head back and met his eyes.

"I saw a nifty Christmas tree a little ways back. Let's go get it and spend this evening decorating."

"Oh! I'd love to!"

___

BACK AT THE HOUSE, MAC PARKED THE TRUCK OUT OF THE WAY, climbed up on the frame behind the cab and handed Elsie the tree. "We have to rearrange the living room before we can set it up," he called down.

"Fine, let's get to it!" she called back.

By lunch they'd swapped the love seat and the Hide-A-Bed. The tree stood between the relocated love seat and the front door. They stood back and studied the room. "I think the tree would look better in the corner on the other end of the love seat," Elsie suggested.

"That could be," Mac replied, "but it would be too near the fireplace. Who's fixing lunch?"

"You are. It's your house," she teased him.

After lunch, the decorating began in earnest. "Leave the tree kind of thin," he requested.

"Why?"

"Because each of the families bring a few of their own decorations."

"That's neat."

Mac nearly fell off the love seat arm trying to reach the top of the tree to place the star.

"Silly! You should know better," she chastised him.

Mac watched Elsie string garlands laced with tiny lights across his porch between the posts. He smiled as she turned to him.

"Do you like it?"

"Magnificent! I didn't know I was getting such a decorator." He reached out and drew her to him. "My decorations have been a bit bland. You have done wonders with my house. I'm looking forward to next year when it's your house too."

She snuggled into him. "I like Christmas."

Saturday turned clear and cold and they took the horses and dogs to the beach. At first Elsie rode like she hadn't ridden very much or hadn't ridden in a long time. As the afternoon progressed, she grew more and more confident. Finally, she challenged Mac to a horse race back to their starting point. Elsie laughed at the dogs as they raced up and down the sand chasing birds and each other, as well as playing tug-of-war over long pieces of kelp.

That evening in front of a crackling fire, they cuddled, hands around cups of hot cocoa. "Tomorrow, the crunch," Mac commented. "The temptation factor will decrease, but the frustration factor will multiply many times."

"Right," she laughed. They sat in silence a moment until Elsie asked, "Mac, when are we going to look at rings? And how are we going to announce it?"

"I figured Christmas day would be appropriate."

"Tuesday?" she responded like she had news bursting inside her.

"Oh, go call your mother. She already knows I was going to ask you this weekend and is probably dying to find out if I have." He kissed her forehead.

Elsie jerked up. "May I? I'm dying to tell another human."

He grinned, mischief in his voice. "It's good to know I'm one of those rare men with a human mother-in-law." He pretended to ward off a blow. Elsie just glared at him. "We can announce it at church Sunday morning too, if you'd like."

She took a deep breath. "Oh you! Give me your cup, and I'll take it to the kitchen. Then I'll call Mother. You're right, I bet she is on pins and needles wondering." She stood and reached for his cup.

About halfway to the kitchen, Mac called after her. "Oh, tell your father, he doesn't have to break out the shotgun." He paused. "Yet."

They both laughed and Elsie disappeared into the kitchen. A few minutes later she stuck her head around the corner. "Mother wants to know when we're getting married."

"Not later than June 19 or 20," he called back. She looked at him in startled silence a moment, then turned back to the telephone with a quizzical look on her face.

When he knew she was occupied on the phone and out of sight, he slipped a little gold box deep into the boughs of the Christmas tree.

CHAPTER 14

Sunday morning, Mac and Elsie made it to church. Elsie winced at his red velour tie. "Ah, let me wear it. I want to tease the pastor's wife today."

Elsie blushed when Mac introduced her to the congregation, but they laughed with her as they congratulated them both. True to form, the pastor's wife, a tiny mite of a lady a few years younger than Mac, tugged at his tie. "Mac," she teased him, her eyes twinkling, "I thought you'd given up this tie. It clashes with your white socks."

"No, it doesn't," he teased back as he lifted one foot and exposed his sock. Elsie winced and covered her eyes. "See, the red stripes on top match the tie perfectly." He grinned at her, as he set his foot down. The small crowd watching roared with laughter.

Not even the pastor's wife could restrain her giggles. "One for you. How's the weather up there?"

"Not bad. But it's time you found out." He reached his big hands around her tiny waist and easily lofted her to one wide shoulder. "How's the weather up there, Pat?"

"Mac!" she shrieked. "Put me down!"

"Mac!" Elsie echoed. "Put her down!" Elsie sank to a pew and rested her head in her hands. "Answer me Pat. How's the weather up there?" Others joined Elsie in the pews, just because they could no longer stand up and keep laughing.

Mac lifted her off his shoulder and set her on her feet. "You're a special lady, Pat. Thanks for letting me do that."

She looked up at him, a little pale. Mac laid a steadying hand on her shoulder. "Mac, don't ever do that again!"

Mac grinned. "Aahh, shucks." A chuckle rolled out. "I won't, but I couldn't resist just once. Besides, I had to get warmed up, my nieces and nephews are coming tonight."

On the way home, Elsie teased him as she complained gently, "Mac, you really embarrassed me after church."

"I'm sorry if I did. Pat and I get along great. She's been teasing me about the weather ever since she and Grant came to the church." He glanced at Elsie. "I won't pick her up again. And I'll even put away my red tie for a season." He grinned at her and she smiled back.

Mac knew he'd been forgiven when Elsie chuckled and said, "She did look a little silly on your shoulder, clinging to your head like a terrified two-year-old." Elsie chuckled again.

They ate a light dinner and started preparing for the descending herd. They settled on ground venison burgers and all the trimmings for supper. Elsie worked on that while Mac moved her things to the loft and spread foam pads for her and the kids. As he flipped out the sleeping bag, he couldn't help but think of cuddling under it the nights they'd nursed Oona.

At 3 o'clock, the dogs announced someone's arrival. Mac glanced out the window. His brother Derik and family had arrived. Derik had barely pulled the trailer next to Mac's outside electrical hookup, when the two older kids burst through the door.

"Uncle Mac," they both shouted as they ran to him in the kitchen, "Do we get to ride in your log truck?"

"Yes, you will. I've scheduled enough loads into Mapleton next week so that everyone who wants can take a ride." He knelt down and gave them both a hug. Only then did they notice Elsie standing next to the sink.

"Who's this, Uncle Mac?" Jessie, his 11-year-old niece, asked, amazed to find someone she didn't know in Mac's kitchen.

Mac glanced up at Elsie. "I'd like you to meet your future Aunt Elsie."

"Aunt Elsie?" echoed a voice from the door. "When did this come about, Mac?" A smaller, black-haired woman stood in the door with a toddler on her hip.

Mac stood and grinned. "You only heard part of it, Marge. To you, future sister-in-law." He turned to Elsie. "Meet Marge McMaridisch. Marge, Elsie Turnupseed."

"Boy, you must be marrying him for more than just the name. Turnupseed isn't much worse than McMaridisch," the teen-age boy retorted.

"David!" Marge hushed her son.

"That's okay," Elsie responded. "He's not wrong."

The adults laughed and Mac introduced the young people. "This is David," he said, laying one big hand on the boy's head. At 14, the slender boy came nearly to Mac's shoulder. "And this is Jessie." He laid his other hand on Jessie. "They're a couple of neat kids, even if they do like to ride in my log truck." He tousled their hair. They laughed, as they swatted his hands away. "And in Mommy's arms is Frances." Mac reached out to the little girl. She smiled, still half asleep and reached out, for him.

Elsie chuckled. "She looks so much smaller in his arms." The other two kids tugged at Mac's elbows. "Can we go out and look around?" they begged.

"It's okay by me. Dress for the weather." David and Jessie disappeared out the back door in a clatter.

A middle-aged man appeared in the door. "So, you let the wild ones loose so soon?" the man said with a smile. Elsie was startled by his appearance. The man was the image of Mac but about eighty percent his size. She was nearly on eye level with him.

"Welcome Derik," Mac laughed, reaching out his free left hand. "Elsie meet my brother, Derik. Derik, meet Elsie Turnupseed, my fiancée."

Derik grinned and shook Elsie's hand. "Welcome to the family, Elsie. We've kind of been wondering when Mac'd find a lady."

Just before supper, Jill and her family arrived. They teased Mac and Elsie about making it official, they'd been suspicious since Thanksgiving.

After gorging themselves at supper, the adults settled around the fire as the kids sorted themselves out as to who would sleep where. The girls chose the loft with Elsie, the boys the trailer with Derik and Marge.

Just before bedtime, Josh, Jill's eight-year-old son, curled up on Mac's lap. "A story, Uncle Mac?" he asked, like he remembered some of the other stories Mac had told.

"Sure, come on." Mac boosted the boy off his lap, then settled cross-legged in front of the fire. The other children joined him in a semi-circle on the bear rug. Frances crawled onto his lap. He started in with how he had met Elsie and their ride to Willamina, dinner with her folks at the house. Then he began the story of their ride to Eugene, making Sam's pursuit of them in his cream-colored Lincoln more mysterious than it had seemed at the time. The confrontation between Sam and 20 other men at the sawmill came out ludicrous to the point of reducing everyone to hearty laughter.

"Is that story true, Uncle Mac?" Janice, Jill's four-year-old asked.

"As true as all my stories." With that response he knew how he'd tell the rest of Elsie's and his fall adventures.

With the kids tucked in, the adults gathered around the breakfast counter on the opposite end of the big room from where the girls in the loft were supposed to be trying to get to sleep.

Not much later, it was just Mac and Elsie in the kitchen. He drew her into an embrace. "Well, do you feel a part of my family?" he asked.

"Oh, yes. Such a neat bunch of people. I'm humbled to be a part of it." She gave him a little squeeze and leaned back in his arms. "You're so good with the little ones. That's neat."

"Thank you." They shared a kiss. "I'm looking forward to sharing our own little ones with you one day." Another kiss. "But it's time for us to crawl in too." He led her out of the kitchen to the ladder set in the bookcase. "Good night, Elsie."

"Good night Mac." As he glanced up, he couldn't help but notice two young heads jerk back.

"Good night to you two also."

"Good night, Uncle Mac," drifted down from the loft. Elsie chuckled.

Elsie climbed the ladder and blew him a kiss from the top. Mac retreated to his room knowing full well that girl talk above him would last long into the night.

CHAPTER 15

On Monday morning, Mac served breakfast as the herd wandered in and sat down. He had prepared pancakes, homemade sausages, the works. Jill settled on a stool at the breakfast counter next to Elsie.

"Do you realize how fortunate you are to get to live here?" she asked with a hint of artificial jealousy.

"I'm only beginning to," Elsie replied with a smile.

After lunch most of the ladies headed into Newport, where they scoured the shops along the bay. The men and boys attacked the load of alder that Mac and Elsie hauled down on Friday. Mac allowed David and Derik to use two smaller chain saws, while he kept the younger boys busy hauling and stacking. Jack handled much of the splitting.

When the women returned, they all wandered to a landing, where they could look out over the hills and forest.

George and Fran were waiting at the house when they returned. Introductions were made once again. Then Elsie and Jill got busy in the kitchen, putting final touches on the venison roast.

After dinner, Mac settled on the bear rug, Elsie beside him, backs to the fire. One by one the younger kids settled around them.

"You got another story, Uncle Mac?" Josh asked like he wasn't sure he should be asking.

"Yeah. Jill, pass me my Bible. It's there on the end table." Jill picked up the maroon covered book and tossed it to him, binding first. He caught it and looked around the circle of youngsters. "What day is tomorrow?"

"CHRISTMAS!!" the youngsters shouted in chorus.

"Why's it important?"

"Presents!"

"Food!"

Typical comments flowed back to him. He smiled. When they'd quieted down, he asked again, "But why is Christmas important?"

"We just told you, Uncle Mac."

"But if you didn't get any presents, would it still be important?"

Silence in the room except for the crackle of the fire and the wind swirled rain outside. Mac flipped through the Bible. He found what he was looking for and glanced around the circle again. "Well?"

"Yes, it would. Or at least it's supposed to be. We'd still get together."

"I'd like to think so," Mac replied, reflecting the quiet of the moment. He paused again, then began. "Luke, Chapter two." So, began the story of the first Christmas. He read it more like he was telling a story. They could feel the exhaustion of a young couple looking for a room in a crowded town. Relief upon finding someplace warm to rest, even if it was a stable. "Think of my barn," Mac interjected. "Even on a night like tonight, it's warm and dry, with lots of dry straw and hay to sleep on. Spread a blanket over a pile of straw, and it's almost comfortable."

"Did they have allergies?" Josh asked.

Mac smiled. "A lot of doctors think most allergies are a fairly recent thing. But maybe not, the Bible doesn't say." The story continued until Mac came to an angelic host singing praises. "That's why we celebrate Christmas. So, you see, it's much more than presents."

"Some people say Christmas started as a pagan holiday. That may very well be true. The way some people celebrate it now, it still is. While we don't know what time of the year Jesus was born, it's important to celebrate His coming. Right?"

"Right, Uncle Mac," Jesse replied.

Mac smiled. "It's late. Go get your stockings for Santa tonight."

At his words, the children sprang into action and in a minute or two returned with decorated Christmas stockings for everyone, including the adults. Mac stood, stretched and retrieved four large fancy decorated red felt ones. One for Elsie, Fran, George and himself, the names embroidered on the top cuff-like edge.

Elsie smiled, and Fran exclaimed, "Oh, Mac! I don't think I've had a Christmas stocking in years!"

"After giving me my best Christmas present ever, I think Santa will be good to you too." They all laughed. The kids hunted up the hooks embedded in the concrete and stonework around the fireplace. Within minutes the stockings were hung on the chimney with care, each hung within reach of its owner. Frances' and Janice's nearest the bottom on each side. Mac's, George's and Derik's nearly out of reach high above the floor. They stood back and laughed.

"Boy! Santa'd better have a big sled tonight," three-year-old Frances commented.

"I'm sure he will," Mac reassured her. He scooped her up and kissed her cheek. "Good night. See you in the morning." Mac boosted her up to the loft. He kissed Elsie when she paused at the bottom of the ladder. "Good night to you too, my dear. Merry Christmas."

"Good night, Mac. Merry Christmas." One by one and two by two, the adults crashed also, until the house was dark and quiet.

Very early and quieter than most 250-pound mice, Mac filled the stockings trying not to waken George and Fran in the Hide-A-Bed. Even so, Fran awoke and rolled over and watched in silence.

Just as he finished, she whispered, "Merry Christmas, Santa Claus. Don't forget your cookies and milk."

Mac jumped, then turned and smiled. "You startled me. Merry Christmas."

After devouring the cookies and milk, he returned to his room and slept until the din of excited children penetrated his sleep.

OPENING PRESENTS AFTER BREAKFAST TURNED INTO ORDERLY, joyous confusion with the kids delivering one present at a time to individuals in the room. When it was all over, Mac looked around. "Elsie," he asked, "you didn't get a small gold package, did you?"

She shook her head. "No. But I got enough."

Mac smiled and beckoned Jenny to him. "Jenny, about halfway up in the tree, there should be a small gold package for Elsie."

Jenny gave him a quizzical look and stepped over to the tree, assisted by her cousin Jessie. A moment later, she stepped back with a tiny gold package in her hand. An adult chuckled, then a quiet, country silence slid over the room.

"Give it to Elsie please," Mac requested.

Jenny placed the tiny package in Elsie's hands. Elsie regarded Mac for a long minute. "Is this why we haven't gone looking for rings yet?" Elsie wondered out loud.

Mac smiled. "Open it, and find out."

He watched as she opened the package as fast as her anxious, trembling fingers would allow. By the time she got the wrapping off, the girls of the family had gathered around her. Jenny squealed and Jessie gasped when Elsie opened the box. Elsie sat and stared a moment, then lifted her eyes to Mac. "Thank you," she whispered. "It's beautiful!" They shared a kiss. One of the girls giggled.

Mac reached and lifted the ring out of the box. "Hold out the correct finger, please," he requested.

She did and he slid the ring on. Mac was right, the sapphire matched her eyes, glowing like they did right then. "If it's too big, we'll have it sized when we go through Florence in the next couple of days."

"Oh no! It's perfect." She swallowed, then met Mac's eyes again, her eyes full of moisture. "Thank you." She threw her arms around his neck landing on his lap. Little Frances toddled over to them and tugged on Mac's trouser leg.

When she finally got his attention, she said, "I want to sit on your lap too." Everyone laughed. Elsie turned to her and smiled.

Just then, Mac tickled Elsie, and she nearly rolled off his lap. He caught her just in time. "Go show off your ring. The others will want to see." She did just that.

He turned to Francis and patted his own legs. "Come on up." The girl climbed up, tucked her shoulder under Mac's arm and snuggled up to his chest. After a couple minutes watching Elsie show off her ring and smiling at the responses, Mac gave Francis a little squeeze and said, "How about you and I go put the finishing touches on dinner?" She looked, smiled and nodded.

Mac placed one arm around Francis, stood and settled her on his hip. Together, they headed for the kitchen.

CHAPTER 16

After dinner, the older kids sorted themselves out for a quiet game of something in the loft, and the little ones took themselves off for a nap on Uncle Mac's big bed after a story. The adults sat around the fire and chitchatted. Elsie and Mac kept pretty much to cuddling on the love seat.

With naps ending, the children began wandering back to the fire. "How about a game?" Jenny asked.

"Which one?"

"How about the flea and the bear?" Josh suggested.

"Sure," Mac replied. He stood and picked up the huge bearskin rug. The adults laughed, as Elsie gave him a startled look. Mac chuckled. "It's kind of a 'pile on Uncle Mac' with a twist. The twist is, I only allow 150 pounds on at a time." The children danced around him as he strode out to the open area in front of the door. There he flipped the bearskin over himself and dropped to his knees. He growled and charged at the nearest clump of nieces and nephews. They scattered, laughing and shrieking. The adults laughed with them.

Mac peeked from under his covering. Three pairs of feet approached from three different directions all of them in stocking feet and walking on tiptoes. He froze. At the last minute, he turned and caught two pairs. They fell laughing into his arms. "You're caught," he teased Jenny and David. He released them but felt a little body land on his back.

"Who's that?" he growled with mock severity.

"Frances," squeaked a little voice.

"Ah, just the right size for an afternoon snack for a 'drizzly' bear." He felt her quiver. Frances received the best ride of the day, clinging for dear life to the fur of the bear rug, bouncing around the room on Mac's back. Finally, he bucked her off and caught her in his arms just before she hit the floor. He kissed her cheek and asked, "You enjoy your ride?"

She nodded her head as she looked at him, pale and big-eyed.

He stood her on her feet and gave her a gentle push out of the way. He'd just caught sight of two more feet creeping up behind him. Mac glanced again. Adult feet. Not kid's feet. Ah! It was Elsie. Mac fumbled around like he didn't know she was coming. Silence in the room, except for a giggle from one of the little girls. A moment before she reached for him, Mac turned and charged, growling his best imitation of an angry grizzly. Elsie gasped as she tumbled into his arms. In a flash, he had her flat on her back under him and the bear skin.

"Gotcha," he whispered just before he dropped to his elbows and they shared a long passionate kiss.

Elsie glowed a deep pink that he could see even in the shadows. She shook her head in quiet realization that she had just met another aspect of her future husband. She liked what she saw. "You!" she replied in a whispered exclamation.

He felt a tentative tap on his back. He growled and glanced out. A pair of little feet scurried away. Mac turned his attention back to Elsie and kissed her cheek. "I think our chaperone is back."

Elsie chuckled as she grinned at him. "I think you're right," she whispered back.

He stood, then helped Elsie up.

As Mac flipped the bear rug back in front of the fireplace, Jill teased Elsie, "I see the 'drizzly' bear got you too."

Elsie smiled back. "In more ways than one."

AFTER SUPPER THEY GATHERED AROUND THE FIRE AGAIN. DAVID stopped in front of Mac and Elsie snuggled together on the love seat. "Have you got another story, Uncle Mac?"

Mac smiled. "Sure do. Have you heard of bigfoot?" The kids' eyes grew wide and Elsie looked at him a little alarmed. Mac winked at her as he rose, stepped over to the bear skin and settled on it. Nieces and nephews gathered in a semi-circle in front of him.

"Well, there's been lots of reports around here of loggers and hunters glimpsing something that can be only described as someone in a big monkey suit or a bigfoot. One logger told us how he came upon footprints leading down a logging road. He told me, 'Mac, those footprints were bigger than yours with your boots on.'" Mac stuck out his slipper-clad foot. "Can you believe it? Footprints bigger than mine?" In the midst of the glow of two lamps turned down low, the flicker of the fire and a worrisome storm blowing around the house, Mac wove a story of Elsie's and his experience as if they were rumors from a third person.

He told of a logger discovering a sasquatch trapped in a small rockslide and helping it out. How another logger found one weak from loss of blood from a gunshot wound and kept it alive only to have a bigger one come and take it from his care in the middle of the night.

With great care, he described someone else's reaction to discovering a great bonfire with dozens of sasquatch dancing around it. The beat of the big drums, how the logger watched frozen with fear and fascination until he smelled something funny and heard a rustling in the woods beside him.

"What happened then, Uncle Mac?" Jenny asked, barely breathing.

"Two big sasquatch jumped out and grabbed him!" Mac hissed, emphasizing his words with a sudden lunge at two of the kids, grabbing their ankles. They screamed and the rest scrambled for their parents. Mac chuckled when even Elsie jumped.

"Then what happened, Uncle Mac?" whispered Josh from his father's lap.

"He said he didn't really remember much. Said they made him drink of a honey- smelling drink out of what he thought was a wooden bowl. Then he passed out and woke up in the bed of his pickup. When he crept back the next morning to where he remembered the fire had been, there was hardly a trace."

"Do you believe all this?" Jessie asked, giving Mac a suspicious look.

Mac shrugged. "If six people you trusted all said they'd seen an accident, and they all come to you independently without consulting each other, you'd probably feel the accident really happened. Wouldn't you?"

Most everyone around the fire nodded.

Mac chuckled. "I have three loads of logs to deliver to Mapleton the next two days. Which ones of you kids over five feet tall would like to ride with me?" Six young hands flew into the air. "Okay, okay. I can haul up to two at a time and Elsie gets one trip." Mac paused taking a dramatic deep breath. "Alone." Mac turned to Jill and Marge. "When do you have to leave?"

"Tomorrow. Mid-afternoon would be fine," Jill replied.

"Thursday morning," Marge answered.

"Okay. Can you three decide who's riding with who?" Three of the six kids nodded. "Good, go into the guest room and come out when you've decided."

At six the next morning, Jenny rode with Mac because her family would be leaving that afternoon. Then the two oldest, David and Jesse, took the afternoon run.

––––––––––

THURSDAY MORNING, IT WAS GEORGE—NOT ELSIE—WHO RODE with Mac to Mapleton and back. Mac figured the ladies wanted to talk.

On Friday morning, Fran and George left for home. Mac and Elsie promised to be at their house for church Sunday, then stay through New Year's.

Mac squeezed Fran's shoulder. "Only if I get to watch one football game New Year's Day."

"Only one?" Fran teased back.

"That's all I'll insist on."

They all laughed and then Mac and Elsie were left in the quiet of the rain.

CHAPTER 17

Winter drizzled on. Mac arranged many a load into Wilamina, as often as possible on Friday and Monday. One damp February Friday afternoon, as he sat waiting outside the school, he watched a boy standing under a covered breezeway in front of the school. The boy seemed to be waiting. At last, Mac caught sight of Elsie heading in his direction. The boy looked up at her and Elsie smiled back. Together they approached his truck.

Mac swung out of the cab and greeted Elsie with an outstretched hand and warm smile.

"Mac, Bobby would like to talk to you," Elsie told him, meeting his eyes. "Just you."

Mac raised his eyebrows, then nodded and looked at the boy. He was probably a third or fourth grader, nine or ten. "Sure." He opened the passenger door and Elsie swung in with a now practiced ease.

Mac squatted in the drizzle in front of the boy and stuck out his hand. "Hi, I'm Mac."

The boy shook his hand, giving Mac's hands a second glance. "I'm Bobby." Bobby swallowed. "Mr. Mac, are you living with Miss Elsie?"

"Living with? Like we're married?"

Bobby nodded. "Bobby," Mac replied, meeting his eyes. "We're not living together." The boy looked up, and Mac smiled at him. "And that won't change until we do get married. Okay?"

Bobby grinned. "Okay!" They shook hands on it, and Bobby sprinted down the sidewalk away from school.

Mac watched him until he disappeared around a corner. Only then did he stride around the front of the truck and swing up into the cab. He and Elsie shared a kiss.

As they drove through the rain toward the coast, Elsie asked, "Mac, how do you feel about wives working outside the home?"

Mac chuckled. "Let me express my opinion by expressing my philosophy behind it." He caressed her hair with his cheek. "First, a husband and wife must work together to build their home. Some jobs the husband is better suited for. Some the wife. But they must work together, to do what is necessary for survival. Second, I believe there is no one better for raising a family's children than the child's parents.

"As I watch my friends, I've noticed that in most homes the wife gets bored being at home all the time, especially before the kids come and after they go to school. In most modern city homes, there simply isn't enough work for the wife that applies to the welfare or survival of the family. Two generations ago, the wife had to kill, pluck and cook the chicken if they wanted chicken for dinner. That took time. At my house Elsie, while I'm not expecting you to kill and pluck dinner, there is a lot of work related to the survival of the family. I don't think you'll get bored."

Elsie chuckled. "No, I don't think I'll get bored. Actually, I think I'll rather enjoy getting back a little more to the land. I know I'll never grow tired of walking in your woods." She laid a hand on his knee and gave it a gentle squeeze. "I'm glad you explained yourself that way."

"Thank you. Sometimes the wife has to bring in a salary, or the family just can't make ends meet. Again, right now, that's not a problem. Currently I'm bringing in more than I spend."

"Do I get a budget?"

"For what?"

"For my part of running our home."

He gave her a quizzical glance, then smiled. "Sure. I hadn't thought of that before. We can go over my books this weekend."

With that, the conversation turned to mundane things, like money and who does what around the house.

One weekend in late April, Mac brought Elsie and Fran to Beaver Creek. Early Saturday morning the three of them started planting the garden. Mac watched with a growing love and affection as Elsie planted peas, beans and other cool weather crops. She planted one end of the garden, while Mac and Fran prepared the other 40 feet away. Fran glanced down at the other end of the garden and stiffened.

"Mac!" she whispered, terror ringing in her voice. "What's that?"

Mac looked up and smiled. Elsie knelt on one side of the row she was working on and Oona squatted facing her. They seemed to be engaged in a serious discussion about the seeds. "Oh, that's Oona, one of the resident sasquatches in the area." He met Fran's eyes. They were wide with fear and her face paler than usual.

"Oona?" she whispered. "You've named them?"

"Oh, no. They named themselves. The only others we've met are Oogla, he's the leader of the band, and Shule, Oona's promised.

Fran gave him a peculiar look, somewhere between disbelief and astonishment. "They won't harm Elsie?"

"Oh no. Between Elsie and I, we've saved Oona's life twice. She and Elsie are very fond of each other. Would you like to meet her?"

Fran swallowed hard at least twice. "Ah … yes. I think."

Mac turned toward Elsie, who was still showing Oona what she was doing. "Elsie," Mac called, loud enough to be heard, but not loud enough to startle Oona.

Elsie and Oona looked up. Oona looked ready to bolt for the woods when she saw Fran, but Elsie touched Oona's arm. "Mother," Elsie explained. Oona nodded as Elsie asked if Fran could come meet her.

Elsie looked up at Mac and Fran and said, "Come on down."

Elsie and Oona stood as Mac and Fran approached. Oona smiled as she met Mac's eyes. But her eyes held an uncertainty, flicking around as Fran approached. Fran's eyes echoed the uncertainty several times over.

Elsie looped her arm around Fran's. "My mother," she said in sasquatch. "Fran."

"FFFFran," Oona repeated, drawing out the "F" like it was a new sound.

Fran nodded and extended her hand. Oona and Fran shook hands like Elsie had taught the young sasquatch.

An alarmed grunt came from the bushes. Oona saluted Elsie and Mac by nodding, and with one long bound, she disappeared into the nearby woods.

The trio stood staring at the place where Oona disappeared. A moment later, Fran leaped to Elsie and wrapped her arms around her daughter's neck. "Oh! I'm so glad you're all right! I didn't know what to think when I saw that creature next to you!"

Elsie chuckled. "Mother, Oona wouldn't harm me, any more than I'd harm her. Though, I've never seen her this close to the road before."

"What was she asking about?" Mac asked as Fran released her daughter.

"She wanted to know what I was doing. When I explained it, she wanted a garden, too. She can't very well work ours, being out in the open like it is."

Mac thought a moment, then shook his head. "No. But I know of an open area higher up that might work."

Elsie's eyes brightened. "Oh, could we show her how?"

"I think so. But let's consider all the ramifications first." Her eyes narrowed as she met Mac's look.

"Yes," she responded almost to herself, "we do have to consider the ramifications, don't we?"

Mac nodded and they all got back to work on the garden. Fran began working next to Elsie, and with all the authority of a mother, she requested Mac work near them both.

GEORGE ARRIVED JUST BEFORE DINNER. AS THEY CHATTED AFTERwards over coffee and tea, Mac commented, as he studied the bottom of his cup, "Well, George, your wife got to meet a sasquatch today."

George's dark eyebrows rose. "Oh?"

Mac nodded and chuckled as Fran paled. "A young sasquatch named Oona visited Elsie while we were working on the garden this morning. Fran wasn't sure what to think."

Mac chuckled again as Fran blushed pink. But Mac noticed George's eyes were on him.

"So, those stories you told at Christmas were true," he commented, suspicious.

Mac nodded and grinned. "For the most part."

"Even the story about that dance?" Fran gasped.

"Yes, except we were dancing."

"Mac!" Fran exclaimed. She turned to Elsie. "You danced with the sasquatch?!"

"Yes, Mother. It was a most interesting and enjoyable night." She smiled. "That honey smelling drink packs a real wallop." She rolled her eyes in remembrance.

Fran gasped again as George responded with a chuckle. "What was it, mead?"

Mac nodded. "I think so. A very primitive mead. It knocked us both out after two bowls of a couple cups each." He chuckled with George.

"Is the one you met today, the one you saved twice?"

"Yes. Her name is Oona. She's quite curious about the ways of the 'hairless ones'"

"Is that what they call you?"

Mac nodded. "That's what they call all humans. They call me Mauk and Elsie, Else."

George chuckled again. Fran sat silent looking from one to the other. "Are you going to anymore dances?"

Mac nodded. "At least one more. They have celebrations on the equinoxes and solstices. We made it to the fall equinox and will attend the summer solstice."

Fran gasped. "Elsie, you really want to do this?"

Elsie smiled at her mother. "Yes, Mother. They're really neat people. As Mac says, we're safer with them than with many humans."

"Do you think we could get pictures of this dance?" George wondered in a quiet voice.

Mac sat deep in thought, long enough to begin to make the others nervous. "Yes," he said finally. "We could get pictures, though I don't think we should." He looked up and met George's eyes. "Elsie and I have a trust with them that could easily be damaged if they discovered the cameras. And they would. They know everything I do in the woods."

George nodded. "Yes, you're right, you can't violate a trust like that."

Silence descended around the table. Finally, Mac spoke up. "My coffee is cold. I'll wash, if I can have some help." He wiggled his eyebrows at Elsie.

She grinned back. "I suppose," she teased him. Together they left George and Fran to wander to the living area and amuse themselves.

CHAPTER 18

Mac and Elsie spent three May weekends in the Linfield College library in McMinnville, then the Oregon State University library in Corvallis researching primitive farming techniques. These techniques required only handmade tools and little or no fertilizer.

Mac closed the notebook one mid-afternoon over Memorial Day weekend. He met Elsie's eyes and sighed. "Well, do you think we can teach Oona how to farm without becoming dependent on us?"

Elsie smiled a tired smile back. "I think so. I'd like to try tanning a hide before I try to teach it."

"I'll slaughter a cow this week and we can tan its hide next weekend."

"Where?"

Mac shrugged." You get the supplies. You'll be more likely to find what you need around here, than I can at the coast."

Elsie nodded. "I'm game." They stood and hand in hand walked out of the library.

"This will be an interesting experiment," Mac commented.

"Yes, it will. Oona was fascinated with the possibility of growing her own food. Apparently, they've raided a garden or two somewhere. She seemed to know what the finished product was."

Mac nodded. "I've seen their tracks around my garden." He chuckled. "Maybe, if they have their own, they won't come around mine."

Elsie chuckled with him. At a traffic light they shared a kiss.

"People will think we're college kids," Elsie commented.

"So? As long as they know we're in love."

"Yeah," Elsie remarked as they wrapped an arm around each other's waist.

———————

A WEEK LATER, FRAN STEPPED INTO HER GARAGE. "YECH! ARE you two sure you have to do this?" She wrinkled her nose.

Elsie looked up from the hide she was tanning. "Yes, Mother." Then she rocked off her knees and stood. "It's kind of frightening to think we may be boosting a culture's technology by many generations. That's why we're moving so slowly. We want to make sure we know how to do it ourselves. You should see some of Mac's projectile points."

Mac stood, too, and stretched. "Well, I think if we let that hide dry, we've got it."

"Good. I'm tired. Besides, there's some wedding plans you need to approve." She winked at him.

Mac grinned. "I wondered how long I could stall and not get involved—until the honeymoon that is."

"You!" Elsie jabbed for his ribs, but he caught her hands and pulled her into an embrace. After a moment, she pushed away a little and looked up at him. "Where are we spending our honeymoon?"

His grin was almost wicked. "Shilo Inn, Newport."

"Oh, neat. Why?"

"I thought, since that was where you were staying when we met, you might like to go back."

She smiled as she looked up at him, then jabbed at his ribs again. They laughed as they walked hand in hand into the house.

———————

WHENEVER MAC MET OTHER LOGGERS AND TRUCKERS, THEY'D tease him. "It's not too late to back out!" or "Where are you spending your honeymoon?"

To the first question, he had some smart comeback that set everyone laughing. The second, he'd answer, "The Newport Shilo Inn."

And in fact, he did make a reservation there and even paid for it. Though, he admitted to himself, he had no intention of making use of it. Oogla may have shown him how to cover his tracks in the woods, but Mac applied his own lessons to his world.

AT HIS PLACE, HE CHECKED THE CALENDAR. TODAY WAS FRIDAY. The wedding was set for Sunday at 2 p.m. at the church in Newport. Elsie'd figured she'd attended there more that winter than anywhere else, so they decided to have it there. Why not? Rehearsal Saturday afternoon. Rehearsal dinner that evening also at the church—potluck. The summer solstice was the next Saturday. He was grateful his log deliveries were well ahead of schedule.

Jill and Derik and their families bunked at his house Saturday night. Elsie and her folks decided to make the 90-minute drive back to Willamina, returning Sunday in time for the wedding.

Sunday morning, Mac slipped out of his place first and made it to early church. Pat threatened to tease him during the wedding service, and he threatened to pick her up and throw her in the baptistery if she did. Everyone around them laughed. Another light-hearted stand-off. As soon as he escaped from the well-wishers after the service, Mac drove his pickup north along the coast to Lincoln City. He left it at a dealer's lot, where he rented a nice, though nondescript, sedan with a front bench seat. Back to Newport after a three-hamburger, drive-in lunch at the Depoe Bay Dairy Queen.

He parked the car behind the chain blocking the back access to the church parking lot at the end of the stub off Nye Street. He took a quick check of the parking lot before he dropped down a slight hill behind the church to the alley, then smiling and whistling, he hurried back to the church and slipped in the basement door at precisely 1:10 p.m.

The first person he ran into was Fran. "Mac!" she squealed, "Where have you been?"

He picked her up and twirled her around twice. "Oh, just taking care of some details of my own." He chuckled as he set her down. She wobbled for a second. Mac laid his hand on her shoulder to steady her, as he glanced around the fellowship hall. "Where's Elsie?"

Fran harrumphed at him. "Waiting for you upstairs—pacing!"

Mac spun and bounded up the stairs three at a time with Fran following behind. Elsie stood, hands behind her back, staring out the glass front doors. He crept up behind her and nibbled the base of her neck.

Elsie squealed, jumped and spun around. Relief glowed in her eyes, then a spit of fire. "Where have you been?" she snapped.

Mac smiled. "Arranging some details on my side." He bent and silenced her protest with a kiss. The kiss grew to be an embarrassment to Fran as Mac and Elsie drew each other close and Mac cradled her head in a classic Hollywood embrace. A camera flash brought them back to reality.

They looked around and blushed.

Fran elbowed her way through the onlookers as only a mother-of-the-bride can. "Come on, Elsie, it's time to dress. You don't want to be late." She seized her daughter's elbow and guided her to the stairs. "I'll bring her back, Mac. And you'd better dress too, young man."

Mac grinned and glanced at his own pants and white shirt. He tugged at the seams of his black jeans. "I went to church in these this morning. You mean I can't get married in them?"

"No! And if I see you dressed like that, I won't let Elsie come down the aisle!"

"Oh, Mother," Elsie chided. "Let's go." Together they disappeared down the stairs.

"Where were you earlier?" Marge asked Mac, suspicion lacing her words.

"Taking care of some details of my own," Mac replied, smiling. "But you heard what my future mother-in-law said, I need to get dressed."

"Are you going to let her boss you around like that?" Derik teased.

"Who, Elsie or Fran?"

"Fran."

"No. At least not after we've made all this official and legal." Mac wiggled his eyebrows. Those around him laughed. Mac and Derik strode off down the hall to their dressing room.

A short time later, Mac, Derik and the pastor stepped to the front of the sanctuary right on cue. Mac grinned at his nieces and nephews. The music changed to the wedding march, and Mac watched Jill start down the aisle. A moment later, Elsie appeared at the back of the sanctuary, and Mac caught his breath.

Her long blonde hair was corralled in a French braid, beautifully coiled in the back. The white dress showed off the fine lines of her shoulders. White puff sleeves clung at her shoulders and set off nicely her long, slender arms. A belt snugged the dress at her slim waist. Yards of white satin and lace hung gracefully from her waist nearly to the floor. It rustled as she began her slow, stately walk on her father's arm to the front of the sanctuary.

The smile she shared with Mac, when she started up the aisle, warmed his heart.

During the ceremony, Mac remembered Jenny and Jessie singing a song that was perfect for the occasion. He patted himself on the back mentally for remembering his vows. They were far easier to say than he thought they would be. And he meant every word.

Mac and Elsie welcomed the gamut of friends, as the reception line crawled through the basement fellowship hall. There were loggers, staff and faculty from Elsie's school and members of the church. Mac and Elsie laughed and chatted with them all.

Toward four o'clock, Elsie leaned on Mac's arm. "I'm ready, love."

They shared a kiss that passed Jenny's approval. "Good. Change, and I'll meet you upstairs to sign some paperwork."

"Okay."

Then Mac slipped up the stairs to change.

A few minutes later, Elsie appeared at the top of the stairs. Mac grinned. She was alone.

"Come, my beloved," he called from the end of the hall by the back door.

She threw him a quizzical look, then wandered over to him. "I thought we had paperwork to sign," she asked as he guided her toward the back door.

He chuckled. "We already have. I needed to get you alone, so, we can make our escape." He held the door for her.

"But why so secretive? Everyone knows we're staying at the Shilo Inn."

A wicked grin spread over his lips. "That's what everyone thinks. Come."

He led her to the back of the parking lot, around the rusty chain. With a flair, Mac opened the door of the rental car.

"Mac! Where's the pickup?" she exclaimed.

He put his finger to her lips. "I'll tell you later. Let's go." He closed her door and jogged around to his. A moment later they were on their way.

She snuggled up beside him, and he caressed the top of her head with his cheek. "That was mean, slipping out like that," she teased him.

Mac chuckled. "I don't think so. I'm a rather private man. I don't like people nosing into my life much. My fuse could burn very short, if we got caught in a shivaree tonight. And I'm big enough that I could hurt people."

"I suppose. But what's everybody going to think when they don't find us at the Shilo Inn?"

"That's their problem. We are registered there. In fact, I paid for a night's lodging. I figure if it throws everyone off the track, it was worth it."

They chuckled together. "Where are we staying?"

"The Channel House in Depoe Bay."

"Oh neat! We've seen it from the highway. I always wondered what it was like inside." They rode in contented silence, rubbing shoulders, sharing their new status. Elsie placed more than one gentle kiss on his cheek. Mac kept watching his rearview mirrors for suspicious traffic behind them. He sighed in relief when none appeared by the time they crested Cape Foulweather, about 10 miles north of Newport.

That night, they kindled their own variety of fires in the night.

Monday morning after breakfast, they traded the rental car for the pickup, surprised Fran by dropping in for lunch, then continued to Hood River with a stop at Multnomah Falls. Tuesday, they were up early and made Klamath Falls by dinner. Wednesday, it was on to Crater Lake, and down to Ashland. After settling into one of Ashland's bed and breakfasts, they went out to dinner and went to see a Shakespearean play at the outdoor Elizabethan Theatre.

On Thursday, they almost missed breakfast, and not necessarily because they overslept. Then they headed up Interstate 5 and had lunch at Sutherland, before heading over the mountains toward the beach. They met Highway 101 at Reedsport and spent the night at the historic Johnson House Bed and Breakfast in Florence.

Friday morning, they nosed around the shops in Old Town Florence, shared lunch at Mo's on the riverfront and headed home. Mac cooked dinner at their home for just the two of them.

Saturday morning, Mac awoke first and watched Elsie sleep, nestled beside him. Her long blonde hair lay on the pillow in delightful disarray. He gave her a gentle squeeze. She cuddled closer and breathed a contented sigh. He laid a soft tender kiss on her forehead and her eyelids fluttered. Another kiss, and he looked into her deep blue eyes. They shared a smile.

"I guess it's not a dream, is it?" she whispered.

"No. We're together now. In our own home." They shared another contented kiss. "Who's cooking breakfast?" he teased her.

Elsie dug her fingers into his ribs. "You are!"

He caught her hands and drew her to him. They lay side-by-side in quiet contentment. "Are you ready for tonight?" Mac asked at last.

"Oh, I think so. It will be fun. I'm looking forward to another night of wild dancing. But let's not get so carried away with the mead."

CHAPTER 19

On Saturday evening, they watched the sunset from a landing near the top of the ridge. Then they turned and walked toward the clearing. "Are you nervous?" Mac wondered out loud.

Elsie looked up at him. "A little, yes. Are you?"

"Yes." They paused as they shared a kiss. "I'm more nervous tonight than I was at our wedding."

"Why?" she asked.

"I'm not really sure, other than we're going into something new. I guess part of it is the way Oogla referred to it, a 'mating dance.' That conjures up all kinds of possibilities in my mind."

They walked in silence along the old logging road. "What did Oogla tell you it was like?"

"Dancing, then they send the new couples off into the woods by themselves."

"Is that why you put sleeping bags in the bed of the pickup?"

"Yes. So, we'd have a place to go."

"Thank you."

They turned off the road onto the indistinct trail to the clearing. Again, they stopped short at the sight of the huge bonfire blazing in the middle of the clearing and the many sasquatch dancing around it. The fire in the night both warmed and chilled their souls.

"There's even more this time!" Elsie whispered. At least a dozen danced around the fire and more sat scattered in the shadows back from the fire. The drums throbbed in their ears. Off to their left, the small cooking fire burned. Mac knew one of his steers was part of the feast.

Elsie tugged at his hand. "There's Oona and Shule!" Together they scurried toward the couple. The four of them joined in a dance Mac and Elsie remembered from the fall before. No break before another followed. Mac and Elsie had no time to sit and rest.

Finally, they stepped out of the circle around the fire during a short break. Elsie settled on the grass. Mac whispered, "I'm going after something to drink." They shared a kiss, and Mac headed toward the small fire. Part way there, he met Oogla. The older sasquatch indicated he already had their drink and a chunk of roast. He also wanted to talk with Mac.

"Mating dance two dances away. Rest well. Long, hard dance. Easy to learn."

Mac nodded. "We ready."

"Good." Oogla handed Mac the wooden bowl and chunk of roast and disappeared in the darkness.

Mac stopped when he returned to where he thought he'd left Elsie. No Elsie. He looked around harder. Ah! There she was. The only light-colored head in the group. Group? Oona and several other smaller sasquatch, probably females were gathered around her. Mac waited several minutes until Elsie returned to him, alone.

Elsie sat silent, staring at the fire as Mac settled beside her again. She cracked a tiny smile as he offered her the bowl of mead. Then she drank. Mac eyed her, asking questions with his look.

She smiled again. "They just told me the mating dance is long and hard. But easy to learn. But very important to last as long as possible."

"Oogla just told me that, except he didn't say it's important to last as long as possible."

"I wonder why."

"Why it's important to last as long as possible?"

Elsie nodded in thought.

Mac shrugged. "We'll do what we can."

By the end of the bowl of mead, they'd nibbled on the roast, and the second dance drew to a close. In the pause, more logs were tossed on the fire, and it flared higher. Then the drums started again. This time, the spectators began clapping in time to the rhythm.

As couples began to sort themselves out, a strange humming rose from around the fire. Mostly low and growl-like, but some higher voices, alto and tenor range. The couples began to gather in two circles around the fire, the ladies to the inside. Mac recognized Oogla with an older female. There was Shule and Oona plus over a dozen more, old and young.

The older couples seemed at ease as they assembled. Many of the younger ones appeared nervous, like he felt just before his wedding started. Then it struck him. That's what this was. A sasquatch wedding or equivalent.

Oona and Shule fell in next to Oogla and his partner. A younger couple stood waiting on their far side. Mac and Elsie stepped into the circle beside Shule and Oona.

Then the dance began. Mac and Elsie struggled half a beat behind everyone else. Each couple circled in what Mac would later call a very close rub-your-partner do-si-do. Then the ladies moved left and the men right one partner. Another, but much looser do-si-do. About halfway around, they caught on. This part of the dance called for an almost teasing, flirtatious attitude toward everyone but your own partner. The tempo started somewhere less than a jog, but faster than a leisurely walk on the beach.

The tempo picked up, little by little.

The second time around the ladies made a half-hearted break through the outer circle. A few cheers and catcalls, as two or three ladies broke through. Elsie didn't even come close. Her escape was particularly half-hearted, and Mac's preventative measures were not.

The couples who'd broken through, separated, sitting on opposite sides of the fire. Mac figured this was like the part of the wedding ceremony where the preacher said if anyone had objections to the marriage, speak now or forever hold your peace.

Mac kind of liked rubbing shoulders and hips and anything else rubbable with Elsie. He merely formally flirted with the lady sasquatches. He knew he'd never be able to stand against any of the males, if they thought he was getting a little too serious.

Another attempted escape and the tempo and intensity kept building. Something in the close contact, the pulsating beat, the vocalizing turned the dance sensuous. Elsie glowed with firelight reflected from the roaring bonfire. Beads of perspiration slid off her forehead, down her cheek and disappeared down her blouse. Mac burned to wipe it all off.

Two more rounds and another half-hearted escape. No one broke through the outer circle. Suddenly the dance changed. The older couples dropped out. For a brief moment, silence, then the beat grew sharper and faster. No clapping or humming. The couples began circling the fire together, arms around each other. Some partners swayed around the fire facing each other, others back to front, the female in the fore, the male caressing her.

"Mac!" Elsie asked. "How are we going to handle this?"

Mac watched a moment, then met Elsie's eyes. "Put your arms around my neck." She did and he looped his arms around her waist. Like a couple in a two-step dance, together they circled the fire.

Faster and faster. Around and around. Pivot, swirl, step out to keep out of the way of other couples. The beat became hypnotic. One couple stumbled and spectators rushed to pull them out of the way.

Mac shook his head and fought being overtaken by the pulsating, soul penetrating, mind numbing rhythm. Elsie stepped in time, pressed close to him. The earthy scent of her perspiration only urged on his male instincts.

Before them, Oona stumbled and Shule picked her up and disappeared into the darkness. Other couples stumbled in their daze and were pulled out of the way. Suddenly Elsie went limp in his arms. He scooped her up and stepped out of the circle.

He stood a moment considering what to do. Oogla touched his elbow. Mac almost dropped Elsie in surprise.

"You, good. Mate now. Meet in forest before next moon."

Mac nodded and smiled. "Thank you. Meet in forest before next moon." He strode to the edge of the clearing. Elsie slowly regained consciousness and shook her head. Mac turned to watch the fire. The last couple collapsed in each other's arms. Had Oogla said 'mate now' with mate as noun or verb?

Elsie groaned. "Where are we?" she moaned.

Mac smiled down at her. "Headed for the pickup."

Elsie smiled without opening her eyes. "Good," she sighed and tightened her grip around his neck. She tipped her head up, and they shared a kiss. It convinced Mac that Oogla intended the verb. He decided that fires in the night come in many forms.

CHAPTER 20

They watched the dawn from the landing where they had watched the sunset the evening before.

"It's amazing," Elsie mused. "Now, I really feel married."

Mac smiled and they shared a kiss. "I hope I didn't treat you too rough last night."

Elsie reached around him and gave him a hug. "No. Last night was special in many ways. I wonder if we'll get an invitation to next year's summer solstice."

Mac chuckled. "We'll see when we get there. At least, we won't have to do the last half of the dance. Meanwhile, we've a home to establish." He enclosed her in his arms and they stood nearly motionless as the sun crowned the ridge and lit up the tree- covered hills before them. The ocean beyond glistened silver.

"It's beautiful, Mac," Elsie sighed.

"Yes. I'm sorry to admit, I'm often working up here at this hour, but only stop long enough for a quick glance." Elsie shivered in his arms. They exchanged a hug. "Come, dear, let's go find some breakfast."

She looked up at him and they shared a smile. "Yes. I guess I am hungry. At least my head doesn't hurt this time."

They both chuckled and Mac helped her into the cab of the pickup. "Breakfast in 30 minutes."

Over breakfast, Mac asked, "What were you and the other ladies talking about last night?"

Elsie blushed and swallowed. "I guess you might say it was kind of like what a mother tells her daughter about her wedding night."

Mac smiled. "Oh. Ladies only."

Elsie shared his grin. "Right."

WITHIN THREE WEEKS, ELSIE AND OONA PLANTED OONA'S garden. And Mac and Shule spent many hours making projectile points. The young sasquatch seemed to have a knack for it. One Saturday, they spent the afternoon cleaning a deer hide and tanning it. Oona, Shule and Oogla took a keen interest and soon had that down too.

SUMMER RACED BY. OFTEN, MAC DROPPED ELSIE OFF AT HER parents' house after his first run to Willamina. Then he stopped for dinner after his second run.

Elsie developed quite a tan from working outside. The garden flourished under her care like never before, and the yard bloomed with flowers. Everything—the whole house, yard and garden—looked cared for and loved.

Sometime in mid-July, Mac thanked Elsie for a delightful meal and excused himself. He hadn't gotten two steps when she barked, "And where to you think you're going, Elisias?"

Mac knew by some male instinct he was in trouble. He turned and smiled at Elsie, glaring at him from her place at the table. "Yes, dear?"

"Don't 'yes, dear' me. Sit down."

Angry loggers, truck drivers and sasquatch never stopped him in his tracks like this delightful lady. Mac settled back in his chair. "Yes, dear?" He smiled at her. A smile started to crack across her face, then spread to a full grin. "I'm sorry I barked at you like that." She reached out her hand and he enclosed it in his own.

"Yes, dear," he chuckled.

"You! We need to straighten things out around here!"

"Oh?" His eyebrows rose.

"Yes. When you lived here alone, you kept it pretty clean and neat, but you've become a slob! Clothes all over the bedroom, and you leave your place at the table a mess! What's come over you?!"

"As far as clothes, you took away the hamper. If you'd like, I'll help clean up after meals." He smiled at her, and she smiled back.

"The hamper is in the utility room. I told you that."

"Please, put it back in the bedroom."

"But it's so heavy, when it's full."

"Then we can either get a smaller one, or I can put casters on the one we have."

She eyed him long enough to begin to make him nervous. "Okay, I guess. Why can't you just take your dirty clothes to the utility room?"

"You know how I sleep. I'm not traipsing around the house like that!"

Elsie tipped her head back and laughed. "Oh, Mac. I love you so!" Mac grinned in relief. "Put casters on the darn thing. But what about helping with dinner?"

"I'll clear the table, and we'll go out for dinner after church every Sunday."

Her kind, gentle, loving smile returned. "I can accept that. But what happens if we have guests Sunday?"

"They can either buy their own, or I'll make it up another night."

"Deal! And it starts now!"

"Huh?"

"Clear the table. You said you would!" She laughed and Mac joined in.

BY MID-AUGUST, THE GARDENS BEGAN TO RETURN THE INVESTment of time and effort. Mac worked beside Elsie and sometimes Fran as they preserved their bounty.

As the fruit in the Willamette Valley ripened, they canned what they could and pigged out on what they couldn't.

Elsie met Mac late one afternoon as he parked his log truck. He was just coming off the hill loaded for his first run of the next day. She had a strangely puzzled look about her as she waited in the kitchen doorway. They shared their greeting kisses and hugs, then leaned back in each other's arms.

"What's up, dear?" Mac asked.

She smiled just a little. "I had a visit from the sheriff's department today. I didn't feel I could answer all their questions, so I said you'd be in about now and for them to come back."

"What about?"

"Oona's garden."

Mac stared at her a moment, then a cynical grin spread across his face. "Oona's garden?! What would they want with that?"

"They said something about seeing it from the air, and while it didn't look like a marijuana crop, they'd like to check it out. What are we going to tell them? We can't just say it's being tended by a sasquatch."

"I suppose not. We'll call it your hill garden. You've been fascinated by the difference of how things grow between the two gardens."

"The truth and nothing but the truth. It's just not necessarily the whole truth."

"Right." They shared another kiss and came up for air when the dogs set up a ruckus announcing someone's arrival. A brown-and-white Lincoln County sheriff's car pulled into view.

Mac walked up to the deputy, as he opened his door and stood. The deputy was a big man by most standards, but Mac towered a good head above him. They exchanged a handshake.

"How may I help you?" Mac asked.

"Well, as you probably know, there's a lot of pot grown in the national forest around here. It's fairly easy to spot from the air and fairly easy to identify. We spotted a cultivated plot high up on your land and we'd like to check it out."

Mac smiled. "Sure. But it's only my wife's hill garden. She's new to the coast and was curious how things would grow up on the ridge as opposed to down here. It's mostly beans, peas, corn and root crops."

The other deputy walked around to the front of the car and Mac introduced himself and Elsie to both men.

"Claude Davis," the first deputy said, shaking Elsie's hand.

"Ed Westmark," the second deputy responded.

"Welcome, gentlemen," Elsie put on her best nurse meets supervisor voice.

Claude was not to be put off. "We'd still like to see the garden, please."

"Sure," Mac replied. "Follow us, my wife and I will take our pickup. The road's pretty good until you get about a half mile from the place." He whistled for the dogs, lowered the tailgate and the dogs leapt into the bed.

In the pickup, Elsie asked, "Mac, what if Oona steps out and shows off her garden? She's so proud of it."

Mac sat thinking. He took a deep breath, then responded. "We'll have to talk to the deputies as we go in. She should hear the strangers and stay out of sight. Besides, you know how the sasquatch and the dogs get along."

Elsie nodded.

Mac parked at the landing nearest the trail to Oona's garden. The four of them paused to gaze out over the hills and mountains before them.

"Mac," Ed commented, "Sometimes I envy you loggers, working out in places like this."

Mac chuckled. "It's hard work. More loggers are killed in the line of duty every year in Oregon than officers. I'm fortunate to be able to work my own land. But come." Mac waved Elsie along in front of him and motioned the officers to follow.

The trail wound along the side of the hill through the forest. Once they scared a deer. Mac thought he glimpsed one of the sasquatch. If Elsie saw it, she made no indication. The deputies continued as if they hadn't seen anything. They didn't understand at all the dogs' panicked bolt back for the pickup.

Three-fourths of a mile in, they broke out into the clearing. On the north side lay the garden, nearly 50-feet square. "There it is," Mac quipped, motioning to the cultivated plot of ground.

The four of them moved to the garden, Elsie gripping Mac's hand.

Claude chuckled. "You're right. Peas, beans, corn, carrots, beets, turnips." He turned and met Mac's eyes. "Sorry to have bothered you."

Mac shrugged. "That's okay, I haven't been up here for a week or two." He stooped and harvested a handful of peas. "Care for a snack, gentlemen?" he asked holding out his hand. "Guaranteed no insecticides."

Claude reached and accepted a few pea pods. They, watched, wary as Ed wandered through the garden itself. All at once he stopped mid-stride and squatted. He spread plants back from the aisle he had been walking in. "Mac," he asked, "what size shoe do you wear?" Elsie squeezed Mac's hand extra hard.

"Fourteen's. Why?"

"There's a footprint here that must be nearly 16-inches long." Claude startled and hurried to where Ed still squatted, studying the ground. Claude knelt, then head-to-head, their eyes met.

"What do you make of it?" Ed asked his partner.

Claude shook his head.

Ed looked up to Mac. "What do you make of it?" There was a curious objectivity in his voice.

Mac inhaled a deep breath. "That, gentlemen, is a sasquatch footprint." Both deputies gasped and bent again to study the footprint.

"You're sure?" Ed asked.

Mac and Elsie nodded.

Ed and Claude met each other's eyes, then turned back to Mac. "Right," Claude chuckled. "Kind of like that hay inside your barn is for your pet unicorn."

The officers stood as one and wandered about the garden, ranging even to the edge of the clearing.

When they returned to Mac and Elsie, Ed asked, "How much do you know about this sasquatch?" The question again came without malice, like a professional investigating a case.

Mac smiled. "A lot more than the vast majority of humans. Let me preface my remarks with this: I don't want a bunch of curiosity seekers wandering my land. I'm working all over it and can't constantly be watching out for trespassers." Both deputies nodded.

"This garden was planted in part by Elsie, but also by a lady sasquatch named Oona. She expressed an interest in growing food for her family. We chose seeds and crops that can easily be dried and stored without any further assistance from us. Oona and her mother have done much of the work here; the weeding and keeping other critters away."

The deputies stared at Mac. Looks between total disbelief and complete fascination covered their faces. Their jaws hung slack.

"That's the honest truth," Elsie added. "I wouldn't be surprised if they're watching us now." Both officers popped the snaps on the straps over the butts of their pistols.

Elsie gasped. Mac chuckled, then turned serious. "Gentlemen, don't worry about your safety, if you keep your weapons in their holsters. Oona has been shot once, and we cannot offer you any guarantee, if you pull your guns—especially if you use them."

The officers relaxed a little and lifted their hands off their pistols. But they didn't strap them back down. Mac heard Else take a deep breath, then sigh in relief.

"Come on. We've shown you everything there is to see." Mac again motioned Elsie along in front of him. "Let's go, gentlemen." The officers snapped the strap on their weapons. Then the four of them headed out along the path. The deputies keeping a nervous watch for anything unusual.

Back at the vehicles, Mac extended his hand to each officer. "Write your report as you see fit but finding one sasquatch footprint is rather thin evidence. And we really are interested in seeing how different crops perform at different altitudes and locations."

The deputies nodded. "Thanks Mac. We were sent to find out if that was a marijuana field. It isn't, and that's what we'll say. Oh, keep the unicorn under wraps, never know what publicity it could bring."

"Thanks. See you guys on the road."

They all laughed. Handshakes around again and the officers climbed back into their car. Mac opened Elsie's door, and they shared a kiss as she slid in. Stepping around to the rear of the pickup, he scratched his dogs and latched the tailgate.

Claude and Ed waved again as they drove off. They disappeared over the rise and around the corner. Elsie threw her arms around Mac's neck.

"That was so close! I hope they don't tell everything you told them."

Mac smiled and kissed her forehead. "I doubt it. They won't say anything damaging."

"I hope not," she sighed. They shared another kiss that fanned the flames of their passion for each other.

Finally, Elsie pulled away and smiled shyly. "I love you."

Mac grinned at her. "And I love you." Then he got in the pickup and headed home.

When they got there, Mac jokingly sniffed the air. "What about dinner?"

"Dinner!" Elsie gasped. She pivoted and bolted for the house.

Mac just smiled. He parked the pickup, let the dogs out of the bed and followed his wife. Women! What would happen next?

CHAPTER 21

O n a Wednesday evening in late August, as they sat savoring their coffee, Mac spoke up. "Elsie, I'd like to take a horseback ride Saturday or Sunday after church."

"Oh? Where to?"

"I call it my Grove of the Elder Statesmen. It's a large stand of old growth. I've never taken you there, and I guess it's time."

"Old growth? I thought you said they logged your land 70 years ago."

Mac nodded. "But this one little corner is hard to get to, and they left it. For that same reason, my father and I never logged it either."

SUNDAY AFTER DINNER, THEY CAME HOME AND CHANGED INTO riding clothes. Then they threw the saddles and packs on their horses and wandered up the main road leading into their forest. A few miles in, Mac guided his horse off the road onto a little used trail making a diagonal slice down the slope.

Elsie hesitated, then followed. On they rode. Elsie lost track of time. Every now and then, Mac would stop and turn in the saddle to make sure she was still behind him. Sometimes she'd be nearly nose-to-tail, other times nearly 50 yards behind.

At last, Mac reigned in and swung off his horse. By the time Elsie caught up with him, he'd pulled the saddle and bags off and had them on the ground beside him. He graciously helped Elsie with hers.

She watched in silence as he pulled the bridles off both horses and slipped halters in their place.

"Why are you staking them out?" Elsie asked.

Mac smiled at her. "Because we may not be back until tomorrow afternoon." He bent and tied the long rope to the horses' halter. "Look around you."

Elsie pivoted, awakening to their surroundings. She sucked in a breath in surprise. Instead of firs up to two feet in diameter like were just behind their house, here were firs and hemlock barely her height. Mixed in were alder and assorted underbrush, all fighting for sunlight.

"This isn't your special grove is it?"

"No. I logged this area about five years ago."

"When will it be ready to harvest again?"

"Between 30 and 60 years from now." He said it in such a matter-of fact-tone that Elsie turned to him.

"Then we won't be around to see it."

Mac tipped his head as he shouldered the backpack. "No, I guess not. I'm 33 now. In 50 years, I would be 83. If I'm around, I probably won't be out here cutting it. But come."

He reached out his hand. When she took hold of it, he guided them down a narrow, overgrown trail. Just a few feet in they shared a kiss, and he gave her a gentle shove ahead.

The trail wandered along a small creek, splashing and gurgling its way to the ocean. Gradually, the small firs and alders gave way to larger firs that looked ready to harvest. Moss grew on the branches, hanging down like little, light-green beards. The trail crunched softly as they walked. The underbrush changed too, because they could now see a fair distance under the trees.

Elsie stopped where the trail branched, one continuing up alongside the creek, the other crossing on a moss-covered log bridge with a handrail on one side. When she looked up at Mac, he smiled. "Which way?" Elsie asked.

"Straight on up. We're almost there."

"Where does that path go?" Elsie asked, pointing to the bridge.

"Our family cemetery. We'll stop there on our way back."

They continued on, the trail keeping a steady, easy grade. Elsie listened to the forest around her. As Mac had said, the forest was quiet but never silent. There was the pad of their footsteps, calls of a dozen different kinds of birds, the little noises of the creek beside them, the wind in the trees high above.

At every wide spot they walked side by side, arms around each other's waist.

After 30 minutes in, the trail petered out and Mac stopped. As he set down the pack, he told Elsie, "This is it. My Grove of the Elder Statesmen." He took a deep breath and let it out in a sigh. "If I could live anywhere I wanted, I would live here." Elsie nodded, absorbed by their surroundings. All around her were trees six, eight even ten feet in diameter. Their branches started 20 to 30 feet above her. Moss and fir needles covered the ground. A little bit up the hill, the stream bubbled out from under a log.

"Mac!" she whispered, as she turned around and around looking up at the trees. "I know why you like it here. It's so peaceful. I've never been anywhere like this."

When at last she stopped turning, she walked over to Mac and settled on a log beside him. "Elsie," he began in a near whisper, as if to speak louder would break a spell of some sort, "I want this to stay like this always."

"I think I can understand, Mac. To harvest this would seem almost a crime."

He chuckled, almost to himself. "When this land was first logged, this area was too hard to get to. Even now, it's not easy. Though if I wanted to, I could. But you know what's ironic? It won't be harvested now, because there aren't many mills that can handle trees this big. The nearest one is Noti or Cottage Grove. I can't economically harvest these trees." He motioned to one of the larger trees across the creek. "That one is hollow. Rotted out inside." He motioned to the one next to them. "This one is probably 800 years old."

"How do you know, Mac?" Elsie interrupted.

"Years ago, Dad and I had them cored. Then, there were mills that would pay good money for trees like this, and we were thinking of trying to harvest them. But neither one of us had the heart."

"I'm glad." she snuggled closer. "There are those who say loggers have no heart about trees. They see them as a crop, like a farmer would see wheat."

"Thank you, Elsie." They shared a kiss. "But this may someday be our retirement."

"How so?" She leaned away from him and met his eyes.

"There is little old growth left in this area. Perhaps someday we can charge for people to come here to unwind, to study old-growth forests, to experience the awesomeness of this place."

"Is that why you brought me up here? To see another aspect of our land?"

"In part, but also to share my emotions that are tied up here. There's a lot here that cannot be shared in words, but only by being here and experiencing it."

"Thank you, Mac."

"You're very welcome." They shared another kiss.

Mac stood and opened the backpack. He lifted out a blanket and spread it on a sunlit, needle-padded, level piece of ground.

When he stepped in front of Elsie, he reached out his hands. "Come, my beloved." She reached up, and he pulled her to him. He swept her off her feet and carried her to the blanket. When she realized his intensions, her mild protests turned to joyful celebration.

CHAPTER 22

When their fires for each other cooled, Mac looked deep into her blue eyes. "Thank you, Elsie."

She smiled. "It seems almost sinful to love you out in the open like this."

"But it isn't, is it."

She shook her head no, and they shared a kiss. Mac stood and stretched, then pulled Elsie up to him. "Come." He gave a little tug.

"But our clothes!" she exclaimed, looking around.

Mac smiled at her. "Okay, wrap them in the blanket and bring them. I'll bring the pack."

Elsie gave him a peculiar look, then bent to her task. A moment later, she followed him another few yards into the forest. Around one huge tree, she stopped. In front of her was a hole in the rock. No, it wasn't a cave. It was a tiny rock shelter. Mac opened the door, ducking his head as he stepped in. His look invited her to follow.

Inside smelled a little of mold. As her eyes adjusted to the darkness, Mac lit an ancient oil lamp. "Is that better?"

She nodded, glancing around the room. To the right on the end wall was a large bed a couple of feet off the floor, or at least a platform that could serve as a bed. A potbellied stove stood in the corner, a small stack of wood at its feet. The oil lamp sat on a wooden shelf above a rough built sturdy table beside the door. The only opening seemed to be a window in the door. "Do you like it?" Mac asked.

"In its own way, very much. What is it?"

"Years ago, Dad and I built it to escape to, now and then. I haven't been out here for at least five years or so."

Elsie shivered. "You're cold, dear. Here." He swept the table clear with his forearm, dumped the contents of the blanket on the table and draped the blanket over Elsie. "I'll get a fire going. This place warms up in a hurry."

Moments later, a cheery fire crackled in the little stove, and Elsie had to admit, it did warm up in a hurry. Mac grinned at her and gave her hand a little slap when she tried to get dressed. He requested she help make the bed. Together they rolled out pads and then their extra-long, thick sleeping bags.

Bed made, Mac reached for Elsie and enclosed her in his arms, ending in a classic Hollywood embrace.

Again, they kindled the fires of their love for each other. In the quiet of late afternoon, Elsie lay with her head on Mac's shoulder. "Are we spending the night here?" she asked.

"I'd like to. If you're hungry, I'll fix some dinner."

"Not now. I'd like to look around a bit more before the sun sets." Mac slid out of bed and handed Elsie her clothes.

Outside, they walked around each tree. Elsie lost track of how many there were early on. Finally, they settled on the log they had sat upon earlier. In silence, they watched the day draw to a close and the daytime animals head for their homes.

Then came the nighttime animals. An owl hooted somewhere. Something else screeched overhead. A doe with a fawn wandered up the path until almost in front of them. About 10 feet away, the deer caught their scent and bolted.

As full darkness settled around them, Elsie's head rested on Mac's shoulder and she fell asleep. Feeling a love and affection he'd never felt for anyone else, he lifted her in his arms and carried her back to their hideaway.

In the morning, he had coffee ready for her. They shared a smile as Mac served up bacon and eggs grilled on the top of the stove.

They left the cabin near 9 a.m. and walked quietly, as quiet as the woods around them, back to the little bridge. Mac led the way across and to a level area just beyond it. Barely visible among the undergrowth and small trees were three gravestones. Mac pulled out his hunting knife and whacked away at some of the undergrowth.

The first stone read, Grant Silas McMaridisch, the middle one Sylvia Anne McMaridisch and the third one Brian Giesler McMaridisch.

"The first one is my father. The middle is my mother, and the little one is my youngest brother. As you can see by the stone, he only lived a few days." Elsie nodded. "I was 10 at the time and remember my father talking with the pastor. He said something about having to make the terrible choice of my mother or my brother. My father chose my mother. Brian came home in a little casket. I never even saw him. We buried him before my mother had recovered enough to come home. I remember it was a long time before she laughed again." Mac wiped a tear from his cheek. He pointed to three fir trees just up the hill from the grave markers. "We planted a tree for each of them after we buried each one. Brian's is almost large enough for harvest."

Mac looped one arm around Elsie's shoulders and drew her to him. "Elsie, this is where I want to be buried someday. And I hope you do too."

She looped her arm around his waist and rested her head in the hollow of his shoulder. "Yes, Mac, I can think of no other place more fitting."

They turned to go, and Elsie asked, "Why is the trail so much better to here than the little cabin?"

Mac sighed. "Until just a couple years ago, my brother and sister used to come up here every time they visited."

"Do they want to be buried up here?"

He shrugged. "I don't know. Derik never really enjoyed working the place. Jill loves the woods, but her husband has pretty well trained the woods out of her."

They walked back to the horses in silence, then bridled and saddled them. Back on the road, Elsie brought her horse alongside Mac's. "Where did your parents live?"

"Just down the road a bit. There's an old farmhouse that looks pretty decrepit about a mile before you get to our place."

"It used to be painted white and is kind of L-shaped?"

"That's it. My grandfather homesteaded this area. Dad grew up in that house, just as Derik, Jill and I did. I'm not sure how it all happened, but Dad ended up inheriting a whole bunch of bits and pieces of land around here. Just before he took really ill, we negotiated with the Forest Service and a couple other people to consolidate all our holdings. I got what we have now. Derik got about a hundred acres of valley land, but he just wasn't a farmer and besides this isn't real good farmland. He sold out and moved."

"Did you buy the land from your dad?"

"Kind of. He signed the deed over to me on the condition that I care for them when they couldn't care for themselves anymore. Mom died without warning, when I was about 15. Dad just kind of went downhill for another five years or so, until he wasted away when I was about 20."

Elsie reached out and touched his arm. "Thank you for showing me all this today. And telling me too." They shared a smile and Mac squeezed her hand.

"You're legally family now and needed to know some of our history. Thank you for putting up with me and listening."

"Oh, pooh! I don't put up with you. Race you to the barn." She dug her heels into her horse's side and took off down the road.

Mac smiled. He was forever grateful she was willing to become family. He urged his horse on and caught up with her just before they reached the log barn behind the house. He'd needed to get away with her. Now they could continue on together.

CHAPTER 23

At noon, one mid-September day, Elsie met Mac at the door when he walked in from spending the morning in the woods. They shared a greeting kiss. "How goes your morning?" he asked, meeting her eyes.

"Very well. I got 21 quarts of applesauce done." They shared a smile.

"Good, I like your applesauce."

As they turned, arms around each other's waists, she paused. "Oh, I got a call from the Forest Service. They're going to burn five acres about two miles east of here."

Mac stopped cold. "Where?" he asked.

Elsie looked up at him. "They said about two miles east of here."

"When are they going to touch it off?"

"About noon."

"Today?"

Elsie nodded.

"When's lunch?" he asked sharper than she'd ever heard him.

"Well, in 15 minutes or however long you'd like. Why?"

He turned and faced her, reached out both hands and she reached back. "Elsie, there have been times before that I have had something inside me say move. This is one of them. We need to be ready for the worst. I need to teach you some things."

"Oh?"

"Yes, rudiments like how to run a chain saw, how to drive the Cat and how to run my emergency pump and generator."

"Why?" The sudden urgency in Mac's voice caught her unaware.

"Something within me says be prepared for trouble. As soon as we can, we're going up and start work on my fire line that's between them and us. To do that, you need to know how to run some things. Let's eat as soon as we can. I'll get my stuff ready outside." He drew her to him. They exchanged a hug and kiss. Then Mac strode out the door with a purposeful urgency.

In his shop, he lifted his small chain saws out of their boxes and checked them over. He laid a couple round files and sharpening jigs next to them. Outside, he inspected his water trailer. He just topped off the oil in one of the pump motors when Elsie called him for lunch.

As he jogged across the open area between the shop/barn and the house, the sunlight grew dim. Mac stopped at the back door. Elsie stood in the doorway waiting for him. They shared a kiss. When they pulled apart, Mac motioned to the cloud. "They've lit it off," he commented in a sour tone. A column of smoke rose from the other side of the ridge.

Elsie shivered. "Lunch is ready," she responded.

Over lunch, Elsie asked, "Why the urgency? The Forest Service has burned other clear-cuts around here and you haven't been concerned."

He gave her a slight smile across the table. "I'm always concerned when they touch off a slash burn. Thank Heaven, very, very few of them get away. But the woods are extra dry this year. I think we need to be prepared for the worst."

"You've said that before. And something inside of you telling you that. What do you mean?"

Mac set his fork down on his plate. "Elsie, call it ESP, the gift of prophecy or whatever, but several times in my life, I have had the feeling that I should or shouldn't do something. When I went against that feeling, I ended up in trouble. When I did listen, I came out pretty good and avoided a great deal of trouble." He blushed and smiled at her. "That's one reason I introduced myself that first Sunday we met. Something inside me said, 'Meet that lady.' So, I did. And I'm very glad I did."

Elsie blushed too, then smiled back. "What about tomorrow? Does your 'voice' say something is going to go wrong?"

Mac shrugged. "I don't know. I just feel we need to be prepared for the worst."

"And what is the worst?"

"That this one could get away and come toward us, especially with the east winds we've been having lately."

"So, what are you doing to be prepared?"

"Teach you firefighting."

Elsie's eyebrows shot up and she gasped. "You mean you think the slash burn may get away and come on our property?"

Mac shrugged again. "The odds are against it, but I feel we need to be ready in case it does." Over the rest of lunch, he outlined his plans.

Outside, he had Elsie sharpen the chain on the smallest saw. Then they took it to a leftover alder log. There he instructed her on how to start it and use it. "Remember, when it comes to a choice between injuring you and damaging the saw, damage the saw every time." When he was satisfied that she could operate a saw without risking herself, they moved on to the Cat.

"Whee! This is fun!" she squealed when she got the hang of two-fisted braking to turn the machine.

"Now, back up to the trailer with the big tank on it." Mac pointed to the tank trailer.

"Me?"

"Yes, you."

With the caution of a new driver, she backed the Cat to the trailer. Mac swung off and guided her exactly and hooked it on.

"Now, take it over the bridge, turn around in the road on the other side, then stop just after the trailer is back on this side."

She gave him a peculiar look and headed down the drive toward the repurposed flatcar bridge. "Swing wide turning around," he called as he leapt off the Cat just before it reached the bridge. Elsie sputtered when she realized her coach wouldn't be on board, but she maneuvered everything around fine. She stopped and shut down the Cat where he directed her.

Mac motioned her off the machine. "I have two pumps on this rig." He pointed out the motors and hoses. "One intake and one output."

"Why a pump for output?"

"For pressure to fight fires."

"Oh." Together they hooked up the suction hose to its pump, dropped the free end of the hose into Beaver Creek, started the suction pump and filled the 200-gallon tank. Tank full, he shut down the first pump. "Now," he chuckled, "comes the excitement." Elsie stared at him a moment. "Start the other pump."

With help and encouragement, she did, and water began surging out of the two-inch fabric hose.

"Now, go pick up the nozzle."

She gave him another funny look, stepped over and picked up the hose.

"Great, brace yourself and rotate the front part of the nozzle." Elsie braced herself, but Mac commented, "No, better than that."

She glanced at Mac, then at her feet, spread her feet a little farther apart, rocked a little to anchor herself in the dirt. "That better?"

"Better. Go ahead."

Elsie gave the nozzle a sharp twist, and the next moment, she had a live thing in her hand. The sudden increase in thrust forced her back several paces, and the hose fought to free itself of her grasp. The stream of water wavered off in different directions as she struggled to contain its jet-propelled undulations. Over the hiss of the water, she heard Mac chuckle. The thought crossed her mind to spray him, but she couldn't control this writhing thing in her hands.

Mac stepped beside her. Without words she could hear, he demonstrated how to brace against the force, how to use it to direct the stream where she wanted it. Gradually, she gained the upper hand. She sighed in relief, when the pump motor ceased its screaming and the stream from the hose became a trickle.

"Very good," he complimented her. "Others heavier than you have really been whipped around."

Elsie paled and dropped the hose. Mac hurried to her and caught her just before she hit the ground in a faint.

She came to as he carried her to the house. "Is it all right?" she whispered.

"Is what all right?"

"Did the fire come?"

"No, silly. They just lit it."

"Oh." She shook her head and met his eyes. "I must have passed out."

"You did." He laid her on the lounge, sitting at her waist.

"I guess, I just realized what we're up against."

"That's okay." He bent and they shared a kiss. "Let's always remember what's most important in our lives." His hand swept the room. "All this can be rebuilt. But you," he kissed her again, "can't be."

She reached and pulled him to her. "Yes, Mac. These things can be replaced. But you can't. Thank you." They shared another kiss. "Now what?"

"You rest a minute. I'll get the tools and stuff I think we'll need. Pack a high energy snack, then come outside."

"Okay."

Another kiss and Mac hurried outside.

CHAPTER 24

Mac checked the tools on the tank trailer: hoes, shovels, axes, picks, three chain saws, extra fuel and oil, files. He flipped his hard hat out of the Kenworth onto the stack and carried another hard hat into the house. Mac found Elsie fixing the snacks.

She laughed as she complained about her hairdo, when he fitted the hat to her head. Together they headed out the door. Elsie carried a huge snack bag in one hand. Mac held the five-gallon thermos of water.

The goodies went on the Cat, the water in a clear spot on the tank trailer. "You driving?" he quipped.

"I'd rather not." Elsie blushed.

"Fine." Mac swung up onto the seat, then reached down and helped Elsie up. "Let's go." Mac started the Cat, then put it in gear and they clattered up the road.

"Mac, I've never been in this part of the woods before," Elsie remarked as they rode up one logging road after another, each a little less worn than the last.

"This area won't be ready to harvest for another five years or so. It's kind of my bank account. That's one reason I don't want to lose it."

Elsie nodded, and they rode on in silence.

Finally, they stopped, and Mac shut down the Cat. He pointed up the steep hill at a strip of cleared land about 20 feet wide. Or at least what had been a clear strip several years ago. Now, alders and firs ranging to 15-feet tall fought for sunlight. Underbrush included huckleberries, fern and salal. Nearly a mile farther up the hill, the swath stopped at another road.

"The upper road is the Forest Service's. We need to clear that strip."

Elsie sucked in a quick breath. "All of that!?"

"All of that. Chuck the brush to our side, the left side. Let's go."

He swung off the Cat and lifted out a yellow 14-inch Mini-Mac chain saw, then one slightly larger. Elsie stood beside him and double checked her saw, copying Mac as he worked over his. "Why aren't you using your big one?"

"That's for falling real trees. It's too heavy for what we have to do today."

Elsie nodded. "We're going to clear this all today?"

Mac shook his head. "We can't. I'm ashamed that the fire line has gotten this bad. We'll do what we can. If the slash burn gets away, it shouldn't get here until tomorrow afternoon. Can you smell Toledo? The east wind is up again this afternoon."

Elsie sniffed and nodded. The rotten egg scent of the paper mill hung faintly on the breeze. "Let's work our way up. Cut down everything, alder, fir. If the brush fights you with the chain saw, pass it by, we'll get it later with pruners or brush hook." Elsie nodded. "We'll break when the first saw runs out of gas." Elsie nodded again. Mac fitted earmuffs to his head, then settled his hard hat in place. Elsie followed suit.

He hefted both saws and sprang up the bank. Elsie followed but slower, since she wasn't used to just bounding up steep slopes. Four pulls on each starting rope and Mac had both saws sputtering and snarling. Mac motioned her to start in and turned to the first small tree. Elsie gasped, when she saw how quickly he felled it.

Try as she might, Mac felled three and four trees to her one. At last, his saw sputtered and fell quiet. He stood and flexed his back and shoulder muscles. Elsie's saw still roared and sputtered nearby. Mac smiled at her. Sweat dripped off her forehead. Her blonde hair hung limp and damp around her face. She moved as if tired to the core to the next tree, when her saw sputtered and fell silent. Mac's heart lurched as he watched her sink to the ground, exhausted. She flopped face down, quivering.

Mac stepped beside her and sat at her waist. His hands caressed and massaged her back and shoulders. Several minutes later, the silence overcame the recent roaring, screaming sound of saws and splintering wood. "You've done well, my dear. Very well, indeed," he comforted her.

"Oh, Mac!" she sobbed. "There's so much, and it's just the two of us. We can't get it ready before tomorrow!"

"We will do all we can. Rest. I'll get supplies." With that, he stood, retrieved the gas can, chain oil, snacks, coffee and water jug. "Have some coffee, dear." He held a paper cup out to her. She rolled over and sat up. Together they shared a snack and coffee.

"Rest awhile longer. I'll take care of the saws. Do what you'd like whenever you're ready. What we've cut has to be hauled to the side, some of the brush has to be cut yet. Rest now." They shared a kiss.

Mac turned to ready the saws. Elsie reached for hers and began sharpening the chain. Together they filed and cleaned in preparation for a renewed assault on the fire line. He glanced at Elsie, taking in her tiredness, then refueled the saws, giving Elsie's about three-quarters of a tank.

Elsie lifted her head and sniffed. "Mac! Do you smell that?" she asked in almost a whisper.

Mac glanced at her, then sniffed. "Sasquatch! I wonder who."

The scent grew stronger, but no one came into the cleared area. They heard a rustle in the bushes that would have sounded like the wind to anyone else. Mac grunted out a greeting. "Friends! Mac! Elsie!"

A huge golden-brown sasquatch stepped into the clearing. Mac rose and grunted another greeting in sasquatch.

The creature nodded. "Yune, know you. Why here?" Mac looked up a good foot and a half into Yune's dark eyes.

"Hairless ones in yellow jackets and metal hats light fire at high sun where they cut all the trees. Mauk want to be ready, if fire gets away."

Yune nodded, as his whole body rocked. "Good," he grunted. An instant later, Yune disappeared into the forest.

Mac turned back to Elsie and chuckled at her wide eyes. "He's huge!" she whispered.

Mac nodded. "I thought there were more in these woods. But I don't ever remember seeing Yune before."

"He was at our mating dance but didn't dance."

"Oh."

Elsie chuckled. "Let's get back to work."

"Yes, let's." Moments later they started the saws and they sputtered to life. Then they roared as they bit into wood.

Nearly 40 minutes later, Elsie's saw sputtered to a stop. Two trees later, Mac shut his down. Again, the delightful woodsy quiet settled in around them. Elsie sat, leaning against a large tree at the side of the fire line. Her head was tipped forward and her eyes closed. Mac smiled and checked his pocket watch—5 o'clock. Dinner time. He wandered to where Elsie had set down her saw, picked up both saws and strode off for the cat and trailer. Glancing around, he noted that they had done about a third, at most.

Elsie's exhaustion told him there'd be no more clearing today. Back beside her, he squatted and laid a gentle touch on her shoulder. She flinched and startled awake.

"Oh! Time to get on with it?!" she exclaimed, straightening.

Mac shook his head. "No, we're done for tonight. I don't want to work alone. It's too easy to become careless and have an accident when you're tired."

"Thank you," she responded through her exhaustion.

She accepted his offered hands to help her stand. "Come, it's dinner time." Elsie carried the remains of their snacks. Mac carried the gas can and water. Side by side, they walked back to the Cat.

Elsie sagged against a tread. "And we've got to be back here tomorrow!" Her exhaustion edged her voice. Mac helped her onto the Cat. He blocked the wheels of the trailer and pulled the hitch pin. Over the rumble of the engine she asked, "How do you do it every day? I'm tuckered out."

Mac kissed her on her cheek. "I'm tired too. I don't normally swing a chain saw as much as we have today. It's been a long afternoon."

Elsie took a deep breath and nodded.

When they walked in, the phone was jangling. Mac answered it. When he replaced the hand set in the cradle, he turned to Elsie. "It got away," he remarked with a resigned sigh. "It got away."

CHAPTER 25

Elsie sagged against the counter. "Now what?"

Mac stepped over to her and enclosed her in his arms. "We eat, then rest."

"Okay." She gave him a quick hug. Together, they prepared a simple but hearty dinner. Elsie ate almost as much as Mac when they dug in. She laughed, "Now I know how you can eat so much and not gain a pound. You work it off!"

As they cleaned up, Mac commented, "Let's get back on it by dawn tomorrow."

"Which is?"

"Between 6. and 6:30 a.m. That means out of bed by 5 a.m."

Elsie shuddered. "Let's fix snacks and lunch now."

"Good idea. Then I'll resupply the Cat."

Bedtime came early and sleep almost an instant later.

MAC AWOKE WITH A START, HIS HEART THUDDING WITHIN HIM. Elsie lay beside him, arms around his chest, nearly squeezing his breath out of him. She lay quivering. "So, it wasn't just me," he mused. "But what on earth?" He glanced at the clock—3:15.

Just as his heart began to slow, a sound split the pre-dawn darkness. Not a scream, but it was. Not a wail, but that too. The sound vibrated in his head. It sounded in part like an extra mournful 900-pound coyote in pain. Shivers ran up and down his spine. Elsie jerked and squeezed him tighter. Then he knew what that sound was!

He peeled Elsie's death grip off his chest and flung back the covers. In one leap, he stood beside the clothes he'd laid out for the day. Another second, and he had the jeans on and dashed out the door across to the main road into the woods.

A grunt-growl sounded beside him, and Mac skidded to a stop. He answered, and Oogla stepped out of the brush.

"Hairless one's fire near Mauk's line."

"Thank you. How near?"

"Here to water and again." Oogla raised his arm and pointed toward Beaver Creek.

Two hundred, maybe three hundred yards, Mac figured. "Be there fast!"

Oogla nodded and disappeared into the woods. Mac raced back to the house.

Elsie sat on the edge of the bed rubbing her eyes and shaking her head. She looked up with bleary eyes when he flew back into the room.

"What was that dreadful noise?"

"Oogla's wake up call."

She looked at him like she wasn't seeing or hearing very well. "Oogla? What did he want?"

"The fire is somewhere around two hundred yards from the fire line," Mac replied as he finished dressing.

Elsie snapped awake. "What time is it?"

"It's 3:15 a.m. I'll go start breakfast." They shared a kiss and Mac left her in the bedroom.

———

WHEN THEY ARRIVED AT THE FOOT OF THE FIRE BREAK, MAC glanced up the hill. The first flames flickered several hundred yards away. He sighed in relief, Oogla had underestimated. He reconnected the trailer and turned the whole rig around. "Why?" Elsie asked.

"Because if we need more water, or need to get away, we can head right out, without wasting time." She nodded and paled, more aware of what the worst might be.

Under the light of the rear spotlight, Mac set to work at the trailer. He pulled fire hose up into the fire line. Elsie guided the hose as it came off the reel. They worked in silence, well aware of the increasing aroma of smoke in the air.

With the hose stretched out and ready, Mac pulled out a couple of peculiar backpacks. They looked more like white plastic five-gallon tanks with a pump handle on one side and a sprayer hose on the other. One he filled and slipped on his back. "Let's fit you for the other one. One of us may have to use the sprayer and the other the hose. These backpacks are much more portable. You can cover a lot more ground with them with much less water."

Elsie nodded and Mac assisted her. Her slender shoulders managed to hold half a tank. More than that she struggled maintaining her balance. Mac jogged to the light switch and flicked it off. In the dark, they paused to allow their eyes to adjust to the star-lit, fire-lit, flickering darkness. Mac hefted both chain saws, and they were off up the hill. Elsie carried the lunch and water jug.

At yesterday's stopping point, they laid down their burdens, took off their backpacks. They covered their ears, started their saws and bent to their tasks.

As he worked, Mac grew more and more aware of the flickering, dancing firelight growing ever brighter and closer. The first crackle of fire reached their ears, as their saws sputtered for their first break. A hundred yards through the trees flickered the woods-eating, angry, orange-and-red tongues of flame. Elsie gasped. Mac strode to the backpacks and almost as graceful as a dancer, flipped his on. He grabbed the lunch, the water jug, the gas can and strode back to Elsie.

"What are we going to do now?" Elsie whispered.

"Rest and eat something. This may be our last chance for a few hours." Elsie nodded, pale and wide-eyed. "At least, now, we can see what we're doing."

Moments later, Mac took off the backpack and reached for the saws and sharpened both chains. Between bites, he refueled the saws and topped off the bar oil. Satisfied, he leaned over, and they shared a kiss. "Elsie, put on your backpack, and stay just behind me. Spray out any sparks you see. Let the fire burn right to the edge of the cleared area but no more. If sparks jump the line, either cut the tree down or blow the whistle." He motioned to a police-type whistle dangling on a leather lanyard from the backpack. "If the wind changes and drives the fire across the line, clear out fast!" Mac clamped on his ear protectors and his hard hat, picked up the saw and strode to the edge of the fire line. Moments later, the saw screamed as it ripped into one tree after another.

The fire reached the uphill end of the fire line first. Mac hurried down the slope to his backpack and returned to Elsie. Together, they met the first flames. Sparks bridged the gap to one tree and Mac immediately set at it with the saw. Moments later it crashed across the fire line, its top in flames. He sawed a large section out of the middle to clear a path up the fire line. As he bent to roll it out of the way, six large dark furred hands joined his, and together, they heaved the log out of the way. Mac looked up into the eyes of Oogla, Shule and Yune. Oona stood next to Elsie.

"Help?" Oogla roared over the fire.

"Keep fire on that side!" Mac responded. He quickly cut several large branches, and the sasquatches grabbed them and began beating any flames that encroached on the fire line. Another spark crossed over, and Mac felled that tree. He glanced up. More sasquatch were pulling up the small trees with their bare hands and pitching them out of the way. The slightly larger trees took two. Mac was impressed. He heard Elsie's whistle and hurried to her. Another tree fell out of harm's way. "I'm out of water," she panted.

"Refill from the water jug." They shared a kiss and she hurried down the hill.

Oogla stepped up to him and motioned to the backpack. "I work?"

Mac paused a moment. Of all the sasquatch there, he was closest to Mac's size. Mac nodded, shifted the pack to Oogla and showed him how it worked. He got the idea on the first try, mastering it on the third, then started patrolling up the hill.

Slowly, the fire burned itself out high on the hill and began working its way downward. Elsie shifted her pack to Oona. More than one tree fell to Elsie's chain saw before the tree had a chance to spread sparks any farther on their side of the fire break.

Mac led the woodland firefighting team down the hill, battling the fire as they went. The smoke scorched their throats and stung their eyes. And the heat was fierce. Sweat trickled off his forehead into his eyes. Mac longed to drain the rest of the water jug.

He glanced up. Sasquatch he'd never seen before were beating back flames. In the flickering light they looked even larger and more mysterious than usual. "Lord, let us have enough hose, please," he whispered.

Mac could tell Elsie was tiring. Her motions were becoming more and more mechanical. He chuckled when Oona sprayed her in the face. That seemed to perk her up a little.

A non-human scream wrenched Mac's insides. He glanced up and froze for a moment as four sasquatch tackled another, its hairy arm in flames. Oogla and Oona both rushed to it and sprayed it down. Elsie squatted next to it and checked out the arm. As Mac turned again to the flames, everyone rejoined the fight.

More than once, he jogged to the tank trailer to refill backpacks. With sasquatch using them, they could be filled to capacity. Once as he cleared the top of the bank with both packs full, he saw another flaming snag explode, sending blazing slabs into the fire line. He hurried up the hill to continue to direct the fight.

On a trip to the tank just after dawn, he heard a new sound. He paused a moment. Engines! Big diesel and gas engines crawling up the road. He glanced back. A Forest Service trailer with a big Cat on it crawled around the corner. Behind it came a bus full of people. First, relief flooded over Mac, then a flash of terror. The sasquatch!

Mac whirled, scrambled to the top of the bank, cupped his hands over his mouth and cut loose with the loudest bellow he could muster. "Strangers!" At that instant he was grateful that word seemed designed to travel long distances yet sound much like a coyote howl. He heard the call repeated up the slope. Before the first human firefighter topped the bank, the sasquatch had vanished. Mac sighed in relief. For the sasquatch and for the new help.

He found Elsie collapsed, leaning against a tree, chain saw quiet by her side. Mac squatted beside her. They shared a tender kiss.

"Is it all over?" she asked in a smoke-induced whisper.

"All over but the shouting, since the cavalry arrived in the nick of time. I'll be back in a bit. I need to help." She nodded. They shared another kiss and Mac strode away.

In a half hour, the big Cat cleared a bare swath through the fire break. The firefighters with their grubbing hoes, axes, saws and shovels took care of drifting sparks that settled in the wrong places. Mac worked alongside his human reinforcements. When they reached the end of his hose, Mac fired up the pump and fought the fire with a real stream of water.

By just before noon, the fire had died to smoldering debris on the Forest Service side of the fire break. Tendrils of smoke curled off trees and stumps. The fire crew busily worked mopping up all along the line. Mac wiped his forehead and glanced around. No Elsie. He hopped up on an old stump. Still, he didn't see her. Mac jumped down but before he took a step, a growl-grunt greeting froze him in his tracks. He glanced around. No firefighters watching. Good. He stepped into the woods. Oogla met him.

"Else with us."

"Hurt?" Mac responded in concern.

Oogla shook his head. "Very tired. Where meet?"

Mac thought a moment. "You know where machine is?"

Oogla nodded

"Two turns up road in time takes to walk to my house."

Oogla nodded again and turned to go.

Mac grabbed his shoulder and their eyes met. "Men of forest hurt?" he asked with concern.

Oogla shook his head. "One. Very little. Else and Oona heal."

Mac sighed in relief. "Many, many thanks," His voice full of appreciation for the sasquatch's help. "I lose forest without your help. Thank you."

Oogla smiled. "Forest our home. Mauk, good hairless one." With that, he disappeared deeper into the woods.

Mac stepped out of the woods into the fire break and began gathering his tools. A moment later the supervisor of the fire crew stepped up to him. "Sorry about being so slow, but I didn't think the fire'd get here so fast."

Mac shrugged and the two men shook hands. "You got here before we lost it."

"How'd you do it?"

A smile cracked Mac's grime-and-soot-covered face. "The good Lord provides help in wonderful and mysterious ways."

"Why didn't you use your Cat?"

Mac motioned to the hillside. "The risk of taking my Cat up that hill was greater than fighting the fire without it."

The supervisor nodded, then blanched under his covering of grime and soot. "Still, you and your wife couldn't have done all that yourselves."

"I didn't say we did. I said the good Lord provides help in strange and mysterious ways."

"Where is your wife? She was here when we arrived."

"Resting in the woods. I'll get her."

"Good. You'll get restitution for the trees that had to come down off your land."

Mac chuckled and grinned. "Make sure it comes out of the paycheck of whoever started the slash burn. Maybe, it will teach them to be a little more careful next time." Both men laughed.

"We do prefer not to burn with a northeast wind, but we have to take advantage of a situation when it blows the smoke to sea."

Mac nodded. "Thanks to the bureaucrats in the Valley."

The woods boss smiled. "If you don't mind, I'll leave a few men here to keep an eye on things the rest of today and tonight."

"Great. I was about to insist on it. Thanks for the help." They shook hands again and Mac continued his search for his saw and wandered back to his Cat. Within 30 minutes, all his tools and equipment were accounted for and in place. He again disconnected the trailer, turned the Cat around and clanked up the road.

Relief flooded Mac's heart when he rounded the second turn and saw Elsie perched on an old stump. She turned and smiled at him when she heard the engine. Mac smiled back. She'd pinned her hair back into place with two small, smoothed sticks, her face no longer covered with grime and soot. Time in the quiet forest with Oona had done her good.

As he helped her up onto the Cat, they shared a smile and a kiss. "You're far more rested than I expected."

"Oona insisted I eat something and rest."

"That was wise. Now that you mention it, I haven't eaten much since before dawn. There were more important things on my mind."

"I understand." They shared another kiss as she settled beside him on the seat and they headed down the road to the tank trailer.

They chatted a moment with the crew, while Mac re-connected the tank trailer. As they squeezed by the Forest Service trailer, the D-4 looked toy-like next to the D-8 being loaded. Goodbyes were exchanged, and Mac and Elsie headed down the hill toward home.

"You were magnificent, my dear," Mac commended her. They shared a brief kiss.

"Thank you. When I first saw those flames, I wanted to run and hide." She shook her head. "I can't believe all those sasquatch showed up to help."

"We could have lost the forest, if they hadn't."

"I know. But I also know, I don't want to fight another forest fire for a long time."

"That's only number two in more than ten years. It was by far the worse of the two."

"Good." They rode in companionable silence, gazing at the green around them. After the fire, every green tree and bush seemed even more precious. The clank of the treads and the purr of the engine were the loudest sounds.

Elsie chuckled as she looked around.

"What's on your mind, dear?" Mac asked.

"Oh, do all fires in the night have something to do with sasquatch?"

"No," Mac replied, his voice deep and rumbling as he caressed her hair with his cheek.

Elsie blushed then looked up at him, looping an arm around his waist. "You're right," she whispered. They shared a gentle, loving kiss.

"Elsie," Mac started as he helped her off the Cat at the house, "I'm more grateful than I can say that you were willing to work with me the last couple days. Saying thank you seems so inadequate."

She smiled. "I'm glad I could help. I guess that's part of what it means to be one with your spouse. To be willing to work alongside, whatever the task. I know now what you were talking about before we were married. In a marriage, the couple has to work together for survival."

He pulled her into an embrace. She wrapped her arms around him and nestled her cheek into the hollow of his collar bone. "Elsie, thank you. I love you."

"And I you." They shared a misty kiss that flowed of a forever love.

CHAPTER 26

The rest of fall flew by. Elsie helped Oona dry her produce. Mac, Elsie and Fran joined in preserving the bounty of the "lower garden." Lots of work but good times too.

Elsie persuaded Mac to buy a good cell phone with a pouch that would clip to his belt and a strong, reliable repeater base station for the house. That way, she reasoned, he could call her if something happened to him in the woods.

On rainy fall and winter evenings, they spent cuddling, reading, playing cribbage or other quiet games. The church's younger couples' group met there on a regular basis. One of the men mentioned that Mac grilled venison steaks better than anyone else he'd ever met. Mac chuckled, now knowing why the group was willing to meet at their house.

If Mac thought Elsie had taken root and flourished with all the outside work around the place that summer, she blossomed and bloomed when she conceived late that fall. Her figure filled out, and her skin tone mellowed.

Over Christmas, the family assembled at the house.

"Golly, Aunt Elsie," Jenny commented, "You don't look pregnant!"

The others laughed. "No, Jenny, I probably don't," Elsie replied with a smile. "But I'm a pretty long lady, and we don't show much early on."

The nieces teased her about not sleeping in the loft with them. "Just think, Uncle Mac, next Christmas, you'll have your own flea to play flea on the bear with."

On Christmas Eve, when Mac finished reading/telling the Christmas story, Frances crawled up on Fran's lap. "When Uncle Mac and Aunt Elsie have their baby, you'll be its gramma won't you?"

A little moisture glistened in Fran's eyes. "Yes, Frances, I'll be the baby's gramma," she reassured the youngster on her lap.

Frances sat in thought a moment, staring at the fire. "Would you be my gramma too? Everybody but me and Janice knew our grammas and grampas, but they're gone now. And I'd like a gramma too."

Fran hugged her close. "I'd be more than happy to be your gramma too. And you know something?"

Frances looked up at her and shook her head.

"You know how everyone calls me Fran?" Frances nodded. "My real name is Frances just like yours. So, I'd be happy to have a granddaughter named Frances."

Little Frances' eyes lit up with joy, and she wrapped her arms around Fran. Fran hugged her close.

"Well, Mother," Elsie commented from the bear rug next to Mac, "You wondered why you couldn't find anything for Frances this year."

Fran nodded, wiping a tear off her cheek. Frances looked up. "Why are you crying, Gramma?"

"Because I'm happy." She gave the girl on her lap a hug. "It's very special to be asked to be a gramma, especially by such a special little lady like you."

MAC TILLED UP THE GARDEN SPACE DURING A SHORT DRY SPELL in March. He could tell Elsie was getting eager to get on with planting. A few days later, he met Oogla in the woods. The old sasquatch had a troubled look on his face. They greeted each other in the sasquatch way, growling and rumbling in the native tongue.

"Mauk, bring Else with you next sun." Oogla seemed rather brusque for such a delightful Spring day.

Mac paused, then nodded. "I bring Else. Meet here."

Oogla nodded and bounded into the woods.

Mac shook his head. How could anything that size just disappear into the forest.

Over dinner, Mac told of his brief meeting with Oogla.

"I wonder what he wants?" Elsie mused.

Mac shook his head. "I have no idea. He seemed preoccupied with something."

Elsie met his eyes and smiled. "I'll be happy to come with you tomorrow. I haven't seen Oona much this winter."

EARLY THE NEXT MORNING, MAC PULLED THE OLD KENWORTH up to one of the small roadside log decks. Elsie and he shared a kiss and climbed out of the cab. Elsie dropped to the ground and walked back up the road to where she could look out over the valley. Mac watched her from his seat on the loader. Some women would never enjoy life this far out, but Elsie flourished. He had to chuckle over the difference between Elsie and her mother. Fran didn't mind visiting but being in the middle of the woods bothered her. "All those creatures out there," she'd mutter. Life was good. Very good.

Just as he reached for the controls of the loader, four sasquatch emerged from the woods. Mac startled. There was Shule, Oogla and Oona. Ah! The fourth one was the female who'd danced the mating dance with Oogla. And Oona was pregnant! Her tummy bulged, too! He swung down from the loader and jogged to meet them.

Elsie heard his footsteps and turned to him. She too paused at the sight of four sasquatch. Then she raced to Oona, and the two women threw their arms around each other's necks.

Oogla seemed sad. Shule, somewhat reluctant. Mac greeted them all when he reached them. Oogla laid his hand on the new female next to him. "My mate. Maul."

Mac greeted the sasquatch with all the respect he had within him, using their native tongue. Elsie reached an arm around Maul's shoulders. One quiver ran through Maul's body. Then she smiled a weak, gentle smile at Elsie.

"We leave," Oogla said in a burst.

"Oh no!" Elsie cried.

"We leave," Shule repeated.

"Why?" Mac asked.

"Too good." Oogla continued. "You teach. I teach. We have tools. Grow food. That good. We, men of forest. You, hairless ones. We, never hairless ones. Little one," he motioned to Oona, "must not know hairless ones good."

Elsie stifled a gasp and hugged Oona.

"You return?" Mac asked.

"Maybe." Shule spoke up. "When little one old enough to know difference between Mauk and Else and other hairless ones."

"Thank you for your trust, Shule," Mac countered. "Where go?"

Shule nodded. Oogla pointed southeast. "To forest near big lake in big hole."

Mac nodded, but Elsie looked blank. Mac extended his hand in a human greeting. "You welcome on my land. Safe on my land."

Oogla shook Mac's hand. "Thank you. Maul like here. Next time." They exchanged a sasquatch nod. Mac turned to each of the others. Maul said something as Mac greeted her. He didn't understand it all, but it sounded kind, so he said, "Thank you."

Elsie and Oona shared another tearful hug. And in one leap, the four disappeared.

Elsie and Mac stood staring at the place where they had vanished into the woods and out of their lives. He stepped behind her and wrapped his arms around her. She leaned back on him, and he said, "They were a part of our lives—a very special part of our lives."

Elsie nodded and sighed. "I feel like one of my best friends just walked out of my life." She sniffled and laid her hands on his.

"I think she did. But they're right. From their point of view it would not be good for the little one to grow up knowing us. Just as it will not be good for our little one to think all sasquatch were friends."

"Yes. I suppose you're right." Silence around them, save for the breeze in the top of the firs and some birds singing. Elsie sighed. "May I plant the hill garden?" she asked.

"Yes. Though I don't think the tiller will work through that soil."

"That's okay, I want to plant it like Oona would have. Kind of in her memory."

Mac wiped a tear off her cheek, then one off his own.

"Will we see them again?" she whispered.

"Oona and Shule? I don't know. Oogla and Maul, I think so."

"Good."

"I'd like you to ride with me today. I've got to make two trips into Mapleton."

She turned and faced him. They leaned back in each other's arms. "I'd be glad to come. What about lunch?"

"I have enough to buy it. Besides, I've been kind of slack about taking you out to dinner once a week. We'll hit someplace in Florence about lunch time."

She smiled at him. "That sounds fine. You have been a little delinquent, though you cook enough around the house, so I haven't minded." They shared a kiss.

Hand in hand they walked back toward the truck. "I will miss my talks with Oogla."

"And I my visits with Oona. She was such an eager learner."

Mac stopped short when they reached the truck. "Oh! I haven't even loaded it yet!"

Elsie laughed. "If you don't mind, I'll wait in the cab. I'm getting a little chilled."

They shared a kiss. Then he helped her up to the seat. One quick smile for each other and Mac swung up onto his loader.

───────────

On the way down the hill, Mac asked, "What did Maul say to me?"

Elsie sighed, then smiled as she snuggled next to Mac on the wide seat. "An approximate quote, 'Oona, my baby. Mauk, good mate. Raise little man inside Else to be like Mauk. Family must continue.'" She kissed Mac's cheek.

"A boy huh? That will make your father proud. After all, your mother already has her girl."

"You!" Elsie exclaimed. She waited until they stopped at the stop sign at Highway 101 before she attacked his ribs.

"Oh," Elsie asked, glancing up at Mac, "Where do you think the 'big lake in a big hole' is?"

Mac chuckled. "Crater Lake."

"Oh."

Out on 101, Mac mused on Maul's words. Yes, the family must continue. He could think of no better way than with Elsie. He sighed, content, and caressed the top of Elsie's head with his cheek. Elsie tipped her head and kissed his jaw. Yes, life was good. The ever-growing life within her was living proof of the many different forms of fires in the night.

Made in the USA
Las Vegas, NV
11 March 2022

45407417R00085